THE BEES

Jack Laflin

tempo
books

GROSSET & DUNLAP PUBLISHERS · NEW YORK
A FILMWAYS COMPANY

Acknowledgements

No book can be written without the aid of outside expertise. This one is no exception.

The author is indebted to the following persons and organizations: Edmund Beizer, M.D., F.A.C.A., for his advice on medical terminology and practice; The American Radio Relay League, for information on amateur radio operations; Alphonse Avitable, Associate Professor of Biology, University of Connecticut, Waterbury, for the many helpful insights he provided on bees and beekeeping; Rep. Otis Pike (Dem.-N.Y.), my Princeton classmate, and Rep. William Cotter (Rep.-Ct.), for teaming up in quick action to procure vitally needed United States Department of Agriculture literature from Washington; Pat Pagano, amazingly accurate young meteorologist and former television colleague, for the pertinent weather data he supplied; Lieutenant Biagio Rucci, Commander, Special Services Division of the Investigative Service Bureau, Hartford, Connecticut, Police Department, who provided helpful technical assistance on matters pertaining to the drug scene; and last, but certainly not least, my wife Virginia, who read the rough draft of the manuscript and made many valuable editorial suggestions.

Jack Laflin
Hartford, Ct.
October, 1975

Foreword

The novel you are about to read is fiction. Its characters and situations are figments of the author's imagination.

However, the killer bees, around which the plot revolves, are very much fact.

What happened to change the 9000-year pattern of peaceful coexistence between man and the industrious honeybee? What gradually caused docile, domestic insects whose normal function was to gather honey and pollinate crops to become cantankerous assassins, prone to strike without warning, kill people and animals, spread terror throughout an entire continent?

It began in 1956 with some well-conceived, carefully-planned experiments on the part of a Brazilian entomologist and bee-breeder named Warwick Estevam Kerr of São Paulo. Like many good intentions down through the centuries, this one became merely another milestone on the road to Hell.

Kerr had long admired certain physical characteristics of the African honeybee, *Apis mellifera adansonii,* such as high honey production and heightened breeding qualities. What, Kerr asked himself, would the result be if he cross-bred *adansonii* with the gentle Italian honeybee, *Apis mellifera lingustica,* which formed the backbone of the Brazilian honey industry? At length completely fascinated with the possibilities, Kerr decided to flesh out the skeleton of his thought processes. Accordingly, late in 1956, he imported four dozen African queens into Brazil,

1

of which 26 survived, then proceeded to carry out a series of cross-breeding programs.

While Kerr ultimately obtained a bee that produced anywhere from 30% to 200% more honey per colony than the Italian strain, he was horrified to discover he had spawned in the process an entomological Frankenstein monster.

It works longer than any competitor; it flies higher, faster and farther; it lives longer, proliferates more quickly and produces twice as much honey per colony. Unfortunately, it can also be an aggressive, foul-tempered killer.

As if the mere existence of this flying nightmare weren't sufficiently frightening, in 1957 a visiting beekeeper mistakenly liberated from their hives Kerr's 26 remaining African queens. The ladies in question promptly hightailed it for the tall timber, there to meet, and mate with, *lingustica* drones. Countless generations later, their descendants have spread like a brushfire over much of the South American land mass, hijacking and Africanizing *lingustica* hives wherever they came across them. Brazil, Uruguay, Paraguay, Argentina, parts of Chile and Peru all felt the presence of *adansonii* within their borders.

By 1974, the vicious bees had left panic, devastation and a trail of authenticated attack stories in their wake, as well as 150 known dead human beings and untold thousands of slaughtered animals.

At the beginning of 1975, the 20-year plague unleashed by Warwick Kerr's well-meaning speculations regarding increased honey production had left only Ecuador, Colombia and Venezuela untouched by *adansonii*. They were not destined to remain so, however, for very long.

Spurred to unusual heights of reproductive frenzies through a continuing cycle of devastatingly hot summers and unusually mild winters, the hybrid *adansonii* bees multiplied with incredible rapidity, an apian population explosion the like of which the world had never seen. Measures taken to control the spreading immigrants proved futile; the bees simply bred faster than they could be destroyed.

With food supplies constantly being depleted due to their growing numbers, colony after colony winged in a generally northwestward direction, seeking new sustenance.

January 15, 1977

2600 miles due north of the tangled timber forests of Colombia, where the bees bided temporarily, waiting, gathering strength and numbers, a young black man named Alonzo Cole sat at the kitchen table of a Harlem tenement apartment.

Oblivious to the loud Soul music of Ray Charles and Aretha Franklin bombarding him from radios all over the crumbling building, staring unseeingly at the incessant march of roaches up and down the grimy walls, inhaling the mingled odors of urine, garbage and the other noxious smells of the ghetto, Cole drew the rubber tourniquet taut around his upper arm, injected the contents of a "dime bag" of heroin directly into a vein. Dropping the syringe, he leaned back, savoring as always the first euphoric, jolting rush of the heroin as it raced through his bloodstream, produced almost instantly the desired high.

Now that he was "straight again," as the street argot put it, Cole briefly reflected on his future, tried to project what might lay ahead. He had scored, had ceased to feel so strung out. Then, carefully secreting his "works," he laughed. There was no mirth in it, only bitterness.

"Future, shit," he said aloud. "Who the hell am I kiddin'? Junkie's got no future . . . 'less it's his next fix."

It hadn't always been that way for the lean, hard, ruggedly handsome ex-paratrooper. Nobody'd held him down and forced that first needle into him. He'd come to that decision on his own, when life in Viet Nam had assumed the dark, intolerable tinge of futility. Long before that, a

5

slum kid, a truant, a petty thief, he was a product of his environment, with all the ingrained suspicion and distrust of The Man normal to any ghetto-dwelling teenager.

But almost six years of fighting in a dreary, stinking little country whose natives neither knew nor cared the form of government they lived under had served to solidify Cole's hatreds, had at last led him to seek, and find, the blessed dream world into which drug addicts escaped, leaving harsh reality behind.

As time passed, Alonzo Cole widened his prejudices to include what he considered his natural enemies:—all whites, the military, The Establishment in general, the accident of his birth which had left him poor, relatively uneducated, and black. For lack of a better alternative, Cole had re-enlisted when his assigned tour of duty ended. However the regimentation and boredom of peacetime soldiering had soon caused him to go AWOL and return to lose himself in the teeming human jungle that was Harlem. Had it been worth the effort? He doubted it. In effect, he had simply traded one hell for another.

"On the nod," Cole failed to hear the first knock on his door. The second and third passed unnoticed also. When the fourth smote the wood more insistently, Cole roused himself sufficiently to mutter, "Go 'way, man. Get lost. Le' me alone." The words were slurred, well nigh unintelligible, each dredged up with difficulty as from a great distance.

The rapping continued unabated. With a sigh of resignation, Cole levered himself out of the chair and shuffled toward the door. Throwing it wide, leaning against the jamb for support, blinking stupidly, he surveyed the individual standing outside.

Although deeply tanned and heavily bearded, Cole's visitor was obviously Caucasian, by itself a sufficiently surprising circumstance in this section of New York City at this hour—well past midnight. He wore a maroon beret slanted at a left to right angle across his head. A multicolored jungle camouflage poncho concealed some sort of uniform, but did reveal brownish-colored trousers tucked into a cracked, dusty set of paratrooper boots.

"Yeah?" Cole said in a flat tone of voice.

Brushing drops of rain from his face, the stranger said, "Rotten night out. Goddamn climate changes all the time. Used to snow occasionally in the winter, but no more. You Alonzo Cole?"

"Let me . . . think. Seems like I've heard the name . . . somewhere. That's me, Alonzo . . . Edward . . . Cole. Who're you?"

"Peterson's the handle. *Sergeant* Peterson, to be exact. Can I come in, or does everybody in this dump have to know our business?"

Cole stared at Peterson, through him, past him, not fully convinced he actually existed. Then the word "sergeant" slowly penetrated the drug-induced fog. Sergeant? Of what?

"Got no business . . . with you. You jivin' me? Don't even . . . know you."

"Nobody said you did," Peterson retorted. "It happens we have a mutual friend, George Whitlock."

Whitlock? Who the hell was he? wondered Cole. Sounded familiar, all right. At length, a dim shadow out of his past, Cole conjured up the drifting image, caught it, held it in his hazy mind. George Whitlock. His best buddy in 'Nam, for Christ's sake! A huge, friendly, grinning Soul Brother from Detroit who'd once installed windshields on a Ford assembly line. Together, Cole and Whitlock had zapped gooks and fragged their own officers, saved each other's lives on occasion, drunk and brawled and fought and whored from Quang Tri to Vin Loi.

Cole's drug-disoriented mind struggled to nail down the Peterson-Whitlock connection, finally concluded if Peterson were acquainted with Whitlock, the sergeant must be okay.

"Whitlock! Yeah! Great guy! I . . . remember now. One of the best. Real bad-ass . . . like me. You seen ol' George . . . lately?"

Peterson nodded. "Matter of fact, I have. Last week. Before I left. He's one of my troopers, likewise the one who recommended you. I had four other people to see in

New York on this particular recruiting trip, so I thought I'd kill several birds with one stone."

"You got ... some pair ... of balls," Cole grinned. Movements jerky and awkward, akin to an astronaut floating weightless·in space, Cole set a whiskey bottle and two tumblers out on the kitchen table. "Honky ... traipsin' around Harlem ... after dark. Din' it ever occur to you ... you might ... get yourself snuffed?"

Peterson produced the burnt-down stub of a cigar from his jacket pocket, examined it, clenched it between his teeth unlit.

"I've been a mercenary soldier twenty years, Cole. I've had black, brown, white, yellow and all shades in between come at me with everything from straight razors to Schmeisser machine pistols. You think I taught hand-to-hand combat, all the dirty tricks in the book, for nothing? Hell no. I'm still alive. And I intend to stay that way. Sure, Harlem's tough. But then so were Dienbienphu and Korea and the Congo."

Dreamily, Cole stared at his guest. Who was Peterson, really, and what was he after? Cole arched his eyebrows, extended both hands, palms upward, as if to say, I'm waitin', man, lay it on me.

Peterson regarded him over the rim of his glass. "Ever hear of a guy called Leander Soames?"

Cole considered, shrugged. "Uh-uh. Don't mean ... nothin' to me."

"It will. Hear me out. Soames is a British adventurer who was kicked out of the Limey Commando Forces. He has more money than brains, but that's neither here nor there. He's a restless bastard who believes there are unlimited opportunities available for a man with a private army, all hard-case professionals, using the most modern firepower, well-equipped, trained and led by veterans of a dozen wars. Soames is just about ready to complete his complement, then sell their services to the highest bidder. He might be right. You noticed how many hot spots there are around the world lately?"

Cole began to see the light; fuzzy, diffused, unclear, but a light nonetheless. "Yeah. Lebanon. Portugal. Angola.

Beirut. Eritrea. The Middle East. Somebody's always inna
market . . . for good fightin' men . . . like me. Right now
. . . I could lick a dozen . . . a hundred . . . all by myself."

"That remains to be seen," said Peterson drily. "You
interested? George Whitlock told me you probably would
be, when he joined up."

Cole tried to bring the proposition into focus in his
mind. After a time, he parted the mists enough to perceive in Peterson's offer an element of salvation. Plus an
opportunity to return to the only occupation he really
knew.

In his more lucid moments, Cole readily admitted to
himself he could no longer hack it in New York, for a
variety of reasons. He was unemployed. Broke. Possessed
no discernible civilian skill. Supported a costly monkey on
his back.

Cole fed his habit by burglary, robbery, and Times
Square hustling, a precarious existence at best. He realized he'd been lucky thus far, very lucky in that his criminal activities had escaped police attention; he was helped
by the city's fiscal crunch which took hundreds of pa-
trolmen off streets and subways, thereby reducing even
further his chances of running afoul of the law.

By the same token, his native shrewdness convinced
him it was only a matter of time before some unlucky in-
cident, a confrontation with an undercover cop, the lack
of a fix would land him in the slammer, kicking his heroin
addiction "cold turkey," undergoing the wretched pangs
of withdrawal in shrieking, nauseated, sweating misery.
Cole shuddered at the thought, recalling the numerous in-
stances when he'd tried to kick by himself. If the authorities sent him to the Federal Detoxification Center at Lex-
ington, Kentucky he would fare no better. To these grim
speculations he had appended a third. He knew the
single-minded tenacity of the military. They would never
rest until they birddogged an AWOL soldier and returned
him to face their peculiar double-standard brand of justice.

Why not? he wondered vaguely. What the hell did he

owe the United States, except to shake the dust of it from his feet as quickly as possible?

"I s'pose . . . my arm could be twisted . . . Sarge," Cole drawled. "Mention some numbers . . . With dollar signs in front."

"Standard scale, plus. Soames ain't cheap, because he knows he's got plenty of competition in mercenary recruitment. Thousand a month for privates. Twelve-fifty if you make corporal. Fifteen hundred and up for three stripes, depending on length of service and leadership ability. Cash on the barrelhead, British pounds, U.S. dollars, Swiss francs. Not that you'd get to spend any of it for a while. We're training at a camp in the jungle of eastern Nicaragua. You think you've seen boondocks before? Shit."

Cole nodded sagely several times. "Beautiful. Jungles, green . . . my favorite color . . . Same as money. I dig the jungle. Did you . . . say anything . . . 'bout weapons?"

"Late model stuff," said Peterson, "although not all standardized. For rifles, Russian AK-47's. American M-16's. British 742 Handleys, right off the assembly line. Anti-tank bazookas. Mortars. Flame throwers. Napalm. Some stolen from NATO convoys, the rest bought. Eventually, according to Soames, he'll buy himself an air force. I hear he's dickering for a couple of used MIGs or French Mirages."

Cole forced himself to concentrate on what Peterson was saying, finding it increasingly difficult.

"Sounds . . . okay. I'm ready . . . say yes right now. But you're . . . no idiot. You got eyes. How'm I . . . gonna bury myself in the boondocks?" He bared his left arm to the bicep, showing the needle tracks dotting his sleek black skin. He stood up abruptly, eyes watery. "I'm a junkie. Period."

"So?" Peterson lifted his shoulders in an expressive gesture, seemingly unimpressed. "Big deal. You think Colonel Soames keeps a camp full of lily-white, God-fearing, All-American boys, upstanding citizens who write their mothers every night and hold wienie roasts on alternate Tuesdays? Guess again, Cole. If you can fight, and survive, and chop the other guy up, he don't care if you have three heads. Hell, I've got men in my squad who're on the stuff. It's available even in the jungle, but a hell of a lot purer and cheaper than you'll find out there on Lenox Avenue. Soames has a pipeline from someplace in Nicaragua, and he'll take his cut off the top, but who cares? You got such a great deal here?"

Cole shook his head. He struggled to reach a decision, but thought processes were a lengthy chore. Finally, he extended his hand. "Private Cole reporting for duty ... Sergeant," he said in what he felt was a formal military manner. "Wouldn't be surprised if I made general ... inside three months . . . Bes' fightin' man in whole world ... Nothin' I can't do."

Peterson shook hands with him, sealing the bargain. "We leave tomorrow night, midnight sharp. Private airfield in New Jersey, between Somerville and Woodbridge. A few miles south of Elizabeth. You know the area?"

"Not 'zactly. Give me directions . . . I'll find it."

"Let's drink on it," the sergeant said. To himself he thought, like hell he'll find it. I'll have to come get him to make sure he shows.

Peterson had dealt with hypes before, knew their general unreliability, their euphoria following "shooting up," their lying, whining ways when strung out, their tendency toward forgetfulness, cheating, stealing, even killing for a fix. If Soames allowed them in his group, that was his problem.

Pouring the cheap whiskey down his throat, Cole felt high as the roof of the World Trade Towers, on top of Mount Kilimanjaro. Would this be a new beginning for him? Or the same old ending, exchanging frying pan for fire? Only the passage of time could provide that answer. For openers, Cole assured himself, getting the hell and gone out of New York comprised the key to the whole situation.

January 17-18, 1977

Bucaramanga, Colombia, January 16 (Reuters) —"Terror reigned in this northeastern Colombian city of 225,000 tonight, following an attack by bees of a size and ferocity never before observed in scientific and entomological circles. Eyewitness reports and survivors' accounts are still being evaluated by city officials, but there can be no doubt the attack was sudden and unprovoked, officials emphasized. Fifty-three are known dead, stung to death by angry bee swarms that appeared without warning on the horizon, pouring in from the north. Animals were attacked in similar fashion. One victim, a woman, stung into semiconsciousness, regained her senses in time to save her life by entering a trolley-bus abandoned by its conductor one step ahead of a determined column of bees. Her two children were killed.

"Ministry of Agriculture personnel, rushed to Bucaramanga from the capital city of Bogotá, attributed abnormal bee activity in the region to the frightfully hot weather that has prevailed all over South America, bringing the highest mean temperatures on record. A few dead bees were recovered and already are undergoing exhaustive testing and analysis.

"The dead bees were the largest ever seen, averaging over an inch in length, with commensurately long and powerful stinging barbs. One anonymous government source was quoted as saying, 'Someone has bred a strain of superbees, an African bee

12

which has taken over most South American hives,' but declined to comment further.

"At a hastily-assembled press conference in his Bogotá office, President del Corte assured his countrymen that all possible measures are being, and will be, taken to combat the menace, and prevent a repetition of the bizarre occurrence. He said the bees that terrorized Bucaramanga are being tracked by troops and Ministry of Agriculture workers wearing protective clothing and carrying canisters of smoke and chemical sprays."

[*London Times*, January 18, 1977.]

EXCERPT FROM A NEWSCAST HEARD OVER RADIO BOGOTÁ, 9 P.M., JANUARY 18, 1977 (TRANSLATED FROM THE SPANISH):

"Sixty-one is the latest confirmed death toll in the incredible attack of killer bees on the city of Bucaramanga yesterday morning. Several other persons are in hospitals, critically ill. Some victims, say doctors, were stung as many as a hundred times. President del Corte issued a statement at mid-afternoon today, expressing sympathy with the relatives and families of those who lost their lives, and cautioning against any generalized panic on the part of the Colombian populace."

By newspaper and radio, through the medium of the spoken and written word, many individuals had said many things over the past thirty-six to forty-eight hours in Colombia. Assurances had been made, soothing panaceas offered, the gravity of the situation downplayed to prevent widespread panic. The government had grudgingly doled out facts which had become common knowledge anyhow, but deliberately suppressed others. Such action was deemed necessary, since from the bee attack on Bucaramanga certain highly volatile and unpleasant projections emerged.

ITEM: Scientists had bred a flying juggernaut that, if

unchecked, could become a veritable plague, a scourge on mankind of a scale unmatched since the hordes of Genghis Khan ravaged Asia and Eastern Europe in the 12th and 13th centuries.

ITEM: The expansionist propensities of the giant mutants were fantastic, on the basis of early evidence.

ITEM: Because of their increased size, the ability exhibited by the bees to cover ground had become frighteningly apparent. Simple arithmetic established that parameter. The huge swarm had been sighted previously at Puerto Nariño, approximately 400 miles to the southeast of Bucaramanga. The bees had covered the distance in no more than thirty-nine days, and possibly less. The conclusion thus became inescapable.

The deadly swarm of African hybrid "superbees" was travelling a minimum of ten miles a day.

January 20, 1977

Roy Ramsdell, president and founder of the ultrasophisticated consulting firm known as "Brain Drain, Incorporated," toyed in abstracted fashion with the sole *meunière* on his plate and frowned. Three-martini, two-hour Washington lunches were a goddamn drag, he decided, even if his dining table companions included big shots like Arthur Bemis and Lewis Runk, who might conceivably become clients of his at some distant day in the future. No, all other factors being equal, he knew he'd rather be back in the DeSales Street office (or "think tank," as the press had recently referred to it), feeding relevant data into a computer's memory banks, helping solve weighty problems besetting government and industry.

Only thirty-five, formerly a member of the National Academy of Sciences, Ramsdell was regarded as a brilliant young scientist with a limitless future, the academic leader of one of the more illustrious classes in Cal Tech's history.

There was so much to do, he reminded himself, and so little time in which to do it! Why, then, must he constantly divorce himself from the realm of pure science, which he loved with a passion, to spend time in idle chit-chat, which he loathed in equal degree? Simply because he owed Congressman Frank Stendler a favor. Ramsdell sighed. Such distractions had driven him to fury before he learned transcendental meditation. They were still irritating enough, but it was the way of the world, he guessed. Particularly on the convoluted, ridiculous, double-talking Washington scene, where straightforward answers and a standup approach to people were as rare as Kosher butchers in Kuwait. On the other side of the coin, it was in his work that the energy gained from his daily minutes of meditation found an outlet. Ramsdell's work (as he saw it) permitted no ambiguities, no circumlocutions, no "bureaucratese"; he dealt in solid, concrete concepts, analyzed them for clients, drew conclusions, made recommendations, and that was the end of it.

The latest BDI projects illustrated Ramsdell's thesis. The domestic motorcar industry and the Environmental Protection Agency had jointly sought the firm's services to research alternatives to federal regulations regarding air-quality standards. After eighteen months of study, Ramsdell and his subordinates had concluded that pollution-free and fuel-saving replacements for the standard internal combustion automobile engine could be developed on a commercially feasible basis within ten years, *if* a crash, $10 billion program were initiated. In a lengthy report, BDI had told its clients that substitutes for the internal combustion engine narrowed down to two top possibilities: the familiar turbine engine currently powering jet aircraft, and the virtually unknown Stirling engine, an idea brought to fruition by an obscure Scottish clergyman.

As if one project of such magnitude weren't enough, Ramsdell was simultaneously immersed in delving into a potentially revolutionary magnetic particle called a "monopole," which a University of California physicist and three colleagues had discovered back in 1973. Ramsdell felt certain that, if properly exploited, the "monopole" might have applications in electronics, development of energy sources, tiny motors and generators, even new cancer therapies. But the time span between personal certainty and proven fact might be a year, or more.

Now that the Detroit-EPA project was over, Ramsdell thought, he could devote full attention to the "monopole" and its various possible uses. In addition, if he could get started on—

"Roy, I don't believe you've listened to anything I said in the past ten minutes," Lewis Runk complained, though with a patient smile. He was Chairman of the Board of Albritton Motors, a new entry into the world sports car market. "What far-off cloud is that mind of yours lost in now?" His stomach rumbled; his digestion had been wrecked by the time he made Vice President of Albritton, some fifteen years before.

Ramsdell adjusted his glasses more firmly on the bridge of his nose, ran a hand through unruly black hair before responding. "I didn't mean to be rude, Lew, but you're right, I'm afraid. As to the location of my mind, it was actually up in a balloon above Sioux City, Iowa, with Dr. Buford Price and the group that first discovered and identified the monople. Fantastic damn thing. Has only one magnetic pole, instead of two, so it gives off a magnetic charge. If I can figure out a way to harness it, well. . . ."

Arthur Bemis snorted. It did not make his pockmarked face any more attractive. "Lot of way-out space-age garbage, if you ask me. No offense, Roy, naturally. But as President of Trans-World Oil, I've got other fish to fry. Mainly ways to find new sources of crude. Then, once found, to bring the stuff to customers of Lewis and people like him. That isn't as easy as it sounds, either. Words like 'find' and 'bring' are oversimplifications." Bemis signaled their waiter, held up his coffee cup for a refill.

"I know, of course," said Ramsdell, "that exploration costs are skyrocketing, that Congress legislated the Depletion Allowance out of existence, and that the squeeze the OPEC nations are putting on is giving the word 'oil' a dirty name all over the world. Still and all, when you consider that profits in your industry were up an average 55 percent last year, I don' see. . . ."

"You will in a minute. Hear me out. And I want your promise, both of you, that what I'm about to disclose remains in strictest confidence. The government doesn't want any leaks, at least not at this early stage."

"Okay, you've got it, Art," Ramsdell said.

"Sure, I'll keep my lip buttoned," Runk agreed. "But why the cloak-and-dagger overtones?"

"Because that's the way I've been asked to play it. 'Ordered' might be closer to the truth. The country's assdeep in enough major problems already, without our citizens looking at an ordinary honeybee and seeing a man-killing monster."

"Man-killing monster?" Ramsdell frowned. "What the hell's that supposed to mean?"

"Roy, I'm aware of your reputation. We all are. Your press clippings and bio sketch make Einstein look like a sixth-grade dropout. But let me ask you something. How much do you know about bees?"

Ramsdell laughed. "Are you serious? On a scale of ten, say zero to minus one-half. The last time I even saw one, to the best of my knowledge, was in a prep school biology class. A little out of my line, after all."

"Mine, too," Runk said. He fished out a little silver box and snapped up a pill—like a trout rising to a fly, Ramsdell thought idly. "Launching a new sports car, the auto industry being the way it is, doesn't leave time for much else. Except getting fitted for a straitjacket, maybe."

"Granted, fellows," said Bemis, lowering his voice. "You both can cop out. I can't. Bees cost Trans-World Oil better than $15 million in the past few months alone. More specifically, a vicious specimen known as *adansonii*."

Ramsdell shook his head. "You lost me at the first turn, Art," he said.

"We have heavy investments in Latin and Central America to protect: producing wells, pipelines, exploration teams, the works. These goddamn bees are rampaging around in Colombia now, and we're spending stockholders' money like it was going out of style to safe-guard our properties, research bee-control measures, design protective clothing, offer bonuses to our native workers so they'll stay on the job, plus I don't know what all else. These aren't pennies and nickels and dimes we're playing around with. It's become a costly, ceaseless battle, and some of the best brains in the scientific community have failed so far to come up with a solid solution. At the moment, we're holding our own—barely. But for how long? The Department of Agriculture has never released this figure officially, or any other, but the fact is the *adan-sonii* swarms have the ability to migrate as much as ten miles a day. I have secret reports in my desk right now, under lock and key, that make it mandatory for us to ei-ther contain or destroy these bees. Only problem is, they don't tell us how. The Panama Canal Zone has been men-tioned as the next logical stop-point, but then. . . ."

Runk held up a hand. "Wait a minute, Art. Admittedly my knowledge of bees is equivalent to, say, my expertise on ancient Grecian urns, which adds up to nothing in both cases. But it seems to me I've read somewhere that bees usually fly very low and that they possess limited aerial ability over water. If that's the truth, you've no cause for real alarm, and neither do we. I'm familiar with the topography of Colombia; I was in Bogotá negotiating some export-import agreements just a couple of months ago. The last time I looked, the Andes Mountains were three miles high and the sweetest natural barrier between Colombia and Panama anybody could want. Didn't your experts down there point that out?"

Ramsdell made a writing motion in the air with his hand, calling for the luncheon check. "He's got you there, Art, you'll have to admit."

Bemis turned a flushed countenance toward his two companions. His pockmarks stood out lividly, as they al-ways did when he was upset. "I admit nothing," he said. "Frankly, I think these creatures constitute a real and present threat, to say nothing of the future. They scare the hell out of me. Experts? A pretty shopworn term. Someone once wrote that an expert was a man fortunate enough to guess right in public and wrong in private. Personally, I'm going to keep my eyes open and pray a lot."

Entering a cab to be driven back to DeSales Street, Roy Ramsdell had little or no inkling that a random lunchtime conversation with two captains of industry was about to change the course of his life.

January 25, 1977

In the Presidential Palace at Bogotá, a weary and irritated Ramón del Corte paused in the act of affixing his crabbed signature to a pile of official documents. He ground his dentures.

"Paperwork," he growled. "The true measure of a bureaucracy's ability to make itself seem important." He glanced at his wristwatch. It was 1:23 A.M.

Del Corte's plump executive assistant entered, extended to the Colombian chief of state a brown manila envelope, sealed in three places with heavy wax blobs, bearing the capitalized, underlined, printed words "PARA OJOS SOLAMENTE" ("EYES ONLY"). Motioning his aide to wait, as regulations required, del Corte broke the seals, wondering what new disaster had overtaken his fledgling administration. Three months in office, he told himself, in a country never noted for political stability or presidential tenure, and you've so far survived sufficient crises for a full term. A poor coffee crop. Inflation. Communist agitation. Strikes. Sabre-rattling border incidents, stemming from disputed boundary claims, with both Ecuador and Peru. On top of everything else, *las abejas malditas*.

The accursed bees.

Del Corte fully expected the hand-delivered message to concern them, nor was he mistaken. As he perused the typewritten sheets his sense of alarm and futility grew.

24 JANUARY, 1977 [he read]
FROM: JOSE AZCARRIAGA, MINISTER OF AGRICULTURE
TO: PRESIDENT RAMON DEL CORTE
SUBJ: UPDATE ON BEE CONTROL EFFORTS

1. It is with grave regret that I inform Your Excellency we are losing the battle to save our country from the depredations of the killer bees of the *adansonii* strain. They advance; we retreat. There is no other sane construction this office can place on what is occurring.

2. We have applied every conceivable control technique in an attempt to effect at least a stalemate. We have consulted with military and scientific minds here in our own country. In addition, we have been in communication with such eminent United States experts on apiculture as Norman E. Gary, University of California at Davis; Charles D. Michener, University of Kansas; Marshall Levin, United States Department of Agriculture, Bethesda, Maryland; and Roger Moore, Cornell University. These well-known persons have given freely of their time and expertise, all to no avail thus far.

3. Three major thrusts have constituted our battle plan against the bees—extermination, containment, and flight disruption. We have employed chemical smoke, with the help of the Army; ultrasonic sound waves; aerial applications of sucrose solution containing poison; bee fences; swarm capture; plus several other highly speculative measures suggested by certain German and Canadian bee experts.

4. *Our efforts have failed, or shown but temporary effects*. We attribute these results to many factors: continuing intense heat, which exacerbates the natural aggressiveness and hostility of the insects to a marked degree; heightened resistance of the *adansonii* to chemical toxicants of all kinds;

their greatly increased range, which renders it diffi-cult to mount any sustained offensive in a chosen control area.

5. Experience has demonstrated that our work-ers can operate in bee-occupied sectors only with the use of extremely heavy clothing of a specialized nature. We have found asbestos suits such as those worn by oilwell fire fighters to be useful. However, external temperatures are such that heat exhaustion quickly ensues if this gear must be worn on a sus-tained basis, another factor hampering the work of Agriculture Ministry personnel. In addition, since there is a dearth of these suits in our country, they must be purchased and flown in from the United States and other parts of the world. Already the price of this equipment has more than doubled. It is quite obvious others are already taking advantage of our country's travail.

6. I call your Excellency's attention to the latest reports of bee attacks and outrages at the following points in the past few days: Barrancapermeja, Pamplona, Sogamoso, Chiquinquirá, Aguadas. Thus, while it would appear that scouting parties have broken away from the main body to range north and south, the generalized advance is as a straight line drawn slightly to the north of due west. In short, it is the considered opinion of this Minis-try that the killer bees are heading by the most direct route practicable toward the Colombian-Panamanian border.

7. In view of our lack of success in organizing efficient countermeasures, we can only counsel evac-uation of all populated areas south and west of that portion of our nation contained within map coordi-nates bounded by 5°W. and 75°N. latitude and longitude. To prevent spread of panic and terror over and above what already exists (the death toll now stands officially at 509) we recommend that Your Excellency implement the evacuation order

immediately, to be carried out by Army and Interior Ministry personnel.

SIGNED,
Jose Azcarriaga
Minister of Agriculture

Del Corte leaned back and bellowed. "Get Azcarriaga here by 9 A.M." This time, his secretary in the anteroom could hear his gnashing teeth.

January 27, 1977

JOINT STATEMENT ISSUED BY PRESIDENT RAMON DEL CORTE OF COLOMBIA AND PRESIDENT ENRIQUE SORZA OF PANAMA, FOLLOWING THEIR MEETING IN PANAMA CITY JANUARY 26, 1977 (TRANSLATED FROM THE ORIGINAL SPANISH TEXT):

"For several hundred years, our two nations have shared a common border, heritage, and interests. While we have had our political and ideological differences on occasions in the past, the hour has come for us to stand united against a foe that is clever, tenacious, and deadly. Efforts to combat the menace of the growing bee swarms have proven fruitless. With the help of God and the natural impediments of terrain, we shall continue to hope that the insects' advance can be restricted within the borders of Colombia. We base these hopes on known geographical and entomological facts. One, generally low flight tendencies of the enemy, as attested to by eyewitnesses and survivors of attacks on Bucaramanga and other Colombian cities. Two, limited ability of recognized European bee species to fly over water. However, we emphasize the difficulty of equating the present invaders with European species. Three, the physical presence of the Andes Mountains. We feel these topographical features afford a two-tiered natural defense line: first the mountains, then the vast expanses of the Pacific Ocean and the Gulf of Mexico. While reliance on the God-created barriers will continue, we pledge the pooling of our joint resources to seek new and more effective solutions for the storm-cloud of bees that threatens us all."

February 1, 1977

VIDEOTAPED EXCERPT FROM THE CBS EVENING NEWS IN NEW YORK.

CRONKITE: "As the death toll mounts in north-western Colombia, despite government labors to halt the steady progress of a growing horde of African hybrid bees, news of American lives being lost has reached us tonight. Correspondent Hal Morley reports from Bogotá."

MORLEY: "James McBride, a petroleum geologist employed by Trans-World Oil, became the first verified American casualty in the War Against The Bees. McBride, of Wethersfield, Connecticut, died when swarms of buzzing, hostile bees attacked the small town of El Real, on the Panamanian side of the Colombia-Panama frontier at dawn today. Early radio messages reaching this South American capital left unclear the fate of El Real's other 4,000 inhabitants.

"With the killer bees now demonstrably in Panama, the natural barrier theory involving the Andes Mountains, hopefully expressed by the presidents of Panama and Colombia less than a week ago, obviously holds no further validity. Whether the bees traveled over, under, around, or through the Andes matters not one whit. The fact is, they did. Government scientists and apiculturists I have talked to here in Bogotá were unanimous in their opinion that the new *adansonii* mutants are the largest, widest-ranging, most powerful specimens of *apis* the world has ever experienced. In a dozen or more laboratories at this very moment, dead *adansonii* bees are being dissected, analyzed, and discussed with awe.

"President Sorza of Panama, in a radio broadcast, disclosed plans for evacuation of much of his country, following the lead of the Colombian president. The United States has property and lives to protect in the enclave known as the Canal Zone, which must be considered as the next logical point where defenses may be manned against the bees. What defenses? Manned by whom? This reporter has not been made privy to such information, if indeed it exists. Up to now, Washington continues eloquently silent on this vital point. Hal Morley, CBS News, Bogotá, Colombia."

February 3, 1977

In the District of Columbia, lights burned late in the Oval Office as the President of the United States solicited advice from military and scientific advisors gathered at an emergency session. Top item on the agenda: movement of the raiding bees from Colombia into Panama, and the estimated future course of their itinerary.

Smoke enveloped the room in a thick, purplish haze. A babble of voices, some questioning, other argumentative and contentious, indicated the meeting had proceeded on a far from smooth course. Cries of "Mr. President!" and "My thought on the matter is—" mingled as members of the group of a dozen or so attempted to get individual viewpoints across. At length, the President had had enough— patience never having been one of his fortes. Spare frame partially obscuring the Great Seal of the United States on the wall behind him, the President slammed a palm noisily on the desk top and stood up.

"Gentlemen, it is after three o'clock in the morning. We began our discussions at midnight. I am sorry to note we have made but scant progress, because each of you, as usual, has his own ideas on how to deal with this situation that has so suddenly been thrust upon us. I admit difference of opinion is healthy, but in this instance it is a luxury I cannot afford. Therefore, I beg all of you to give me your undivided attention so I can summarize and we can finish up here and get what sleep we can."

The Oval Office gradually quieted. Chairs scraped as men who had sat too long in one place shifted to more comfortable positions. Carp as the President's political detractors might, even they admitted the tall Ohioan had the knack of zipping together dissident elements, facing squarely unpopular issues others sought to sweep under the rug, calling a spade a spade in uncharacteristically tough language that sometimes caused veteran Washington observers to shudder.

"Let me enumerate what we have covered. If this is all we can agree on in over three hours, the fate of our nation is truly at stake," he said acidly. He held aloft his broad left hand, fingers open, and used the right forefinger to close them, one by one, as he spoke.

"American lives have been lost to these unspeakable insects. Therefore, like it or not, this now automatically becomes our fight, too. The advance of the bees into Panama is an accomplished fact. A unified effort is called for. I therefore propose the creation of an elite group, consisting of the best brains in the various applicable disciplines, to combat a force that currently seems impervious to the most sophisticated control techniques. To head up the group, I nominate a man who has been of invaluable aid to the government in the past, a former member of the National Academy of Sciences. His name is Roy Ramsdell. Many of you here are at least acquainted with him, or if not with him, with his work. He is brilliant, dedicated, personally known to me, and has a reputation for getting things done. I will now allow you ten seconds to place other candidates in nomination. After all, this is a democracy."

As he stared pointedly at his watch, the silence that ensued underscored the generalized sentiment among his subordinates that once the President ran up the storm signals, prudence dictated compromise or retreat. The present situation obviously fell into that category.

"All right, then. It's settled, gentlemen. Roy Ramsdell will be in charge of the new anti-bee operation. Now, to the next order of business. We must prepare for the worst, even though I detest the defeatist attitude involved. If it does indeed occur, it follows that the *adansonii* will overrun Panama, the rest of Central America, Mexico and, ultimately, perish the thought, the United States. I am confident this will not happen. But let's assume it does anyhow; we must be realistic. How much time do we have at our disposal? What are the bees likely to do next, and where? Anson, give us a report, if you please."

The Secretary of Agriculture, Anson Jarvis, hauled his vast bulk to his feet with difficulty. Although the two had differed violently in the past, mostly over Jarvis's oft-repeated contention that farmers walked on water and the American public reacted to soaring food prices like an ungrateful pack of complaining clods, the President realized he'd obtain the bare facts from the obese Jarvis, without sugarcoating or confusing verbiage.

"May I use the wall map and pointer, Mr. President?"

"Of course, Anson. Get on with it."

Clearing his throat, Jarvis began. "Based on what we have observed of the bees' trends and flight patterns since they emerged from the forest around Puerto Nariño, their route is generally on a west-to-northwest axis. It is roughly twelve hundred miles from the Colombian-Panamanian border to the dividing line between Mexico and Guatamala. At their current rate of speed, unless otherwise halted, we project their entry into Mexico by early June of this year. From there, it is another fifteen hundred miles to a point on the Rio Grande River separating Texas and Mexico, in the Laredo-Del Río area. If the bees head in that direction, and of course we have no way of being certain they will, that puts them in or at least near the United States by mid-November of 1977. If for some reason they shift to the northwest, toward California, Arizona, and New Mexico, it might take the bees a week or so longer to arrive. Small comfort, Mr. President, but I'm afraid it's the very best I can do."

"Thank you, Anson. Now we know precisely what we're facing. Nine months and a little more to—well, if not D-Day, then B-Day. I needn't point out that Uncle Sam has confronted difficult challenges in the past and licked them. I hope this challenge proves no exception."

To himself, the President thought, is this *really* me talking? Giving out with the old locker-room, 'Win one for the Gipper' crap? Do I actually believe, deep down in my heart, that Roy Ramsdell, or anyone else, can come up with the answer in that little time? No, I don't, but on the other hand I'd sure as hell better, for the sake of my own peace of mind and the two hundred and ten million people who elected me!

Aloud, he said, "Discussion. Since the Andes range has now been ruled out as a natural defense line, what options are open to us? Andy, your opinions, if you will."

Andrew Mainfort, Commanding General of the U.S. Army Corps of Engineers, three stars glittering on each shoulder, uniform blouse a startling mosaic of campaign ribbons, medals, and decorations, paused to light a fresh cigar.

"The way I see it, Mr. President, the options open to us are few. As a matter of fact, they boil down to one. The Panama Canal Zone. If we can bottle the damn bees up there, or somehow divert them to open water on either side, then I think we might have a chance. Except for that"—Mainfort's shoulders lifted in an expressive shrug—"I'm fresh out of intelligent suggestions. My people can build bridges and move mountains, dredge rivers and lay railroad tracks over swamps. But how much can we be expected to know about bees?"

"Well-taken point, Andy. That's going to be Ramsdell's headache, in double-quick order. Anson, what's your ballpark estimate of the bees' ETA at the Canal Zone?"

Jarvis performed some rapid mental arithmetic. "Twenty days, give or take, Mr. President," he said.

"I see." He stroked his chin. "A tight timetable, but surely not an impossibility if we get cracking on it."

In the next five minutes, the President issued a rapid-fire stream of executive orders, dictating at such speed that his secretary found herself hard pressed to keep pace with him:

Set up a joint conference between himself and the heads of state of Central America and Mexico. Draft plans for total evacuation of Panama, if the need arose. Remove to safety, in any event, those living below and in the Panama Canal Zone. Get Ramsdell and his Brain Drain, Incorporated, crew working on the ultimate problem, the one that seemed capable of engulfing them all. Make certain Ramsdell would have available whatever he required—red-tape-cutting powers, entomological and agricultural specialists, requisitional latitude, unlimited funds on an A-1 priority basis.

At length, a weary Chief Executive dismissed his advisors, asked that black coffee be brought to him, and strode back toward his desk.

Several minutes later, Roy Ramsdell was abruptly jolted out of sound slumber by the jangling of the telephone in his Silver Spring apartment. He fumbled reflexively for his glasses on the bedside table. At the same time, Ramsdell noted it was 4:24 A.M., wondered what nut (in a city chock-full of them) would be calling at such an uncouth hour.

"Ramsdell here," he said.

He recognized the voice on the other end of the line at once.

"Hello, Roy. This is the President. I apologize for the inconvenience. But I need you. So does the country. Can I impose on you to come to the White House immediately?"

"Give me thirty minutes, Mr. President. I'm halfway there."

Ramsdell asked no questions because he felt little doubt regarding the reason behind the note of urgency in the President's tone.

Those South American-Africanized superbees.

Heading toward the shower, Ramsdell vaguely recalled

Arthur Bemis's prophetic words. How had he put it, exactly? Keeping his eyes open and praying a lot.

It wasn't, Ramsdell thought, such a bad philosophy at that.

February 4, 1977

Sitting outside the office of Dr. Sigmund Klein, her United States Public Health Service superior, Laura Messick, M.D., wondered what sort of pest-hole assignment the luck of the draw would send her to next. Not that it made a great deal of difference, she knew; she'd gone into PHS medicine with her eyes wide open—it had offered the best opportunity to carry out the highest ideals of her profession as she conceived them.

While med school, internship, and residency colleagues had indulged in rosy dreams of personal glory and enrichment, wealthy patients, and practices conducted in expensive modern clinics and office suits, Laura's career objectives had followed a vastly dissimilar course.

Ever since childhood, from the first tentative make-believe with dolls and a toy stethoscope, dual ambitions had motivated her: to become a physician, and alleviate the sufferings of humanity. Of the latter, she had seen more than her share in the small Texas town of her birth. Economic deprivation among black and Chicano citizens. Unconscionably high infant mortality. Malnutrition. Diseases that flourished where sanitary arrangements and personal hygiene were often neglected.

Laura Messick could not, would not, close her eyes to the commonplace events that had shaped her medical philosophy. Supplying elderly hypochrondiac ladies with placebos in return for exorbitant fees did not coincide with Laura's concept of fulfilling the Hippocratic Oath. Instead, dedicating herself to the practice of medicine on a broad-based scale, she opted for service in the USPHS. Never for an instant had she regretted that decision.

Dr. Klein opened the office door and beckoned Laura inside. As she entered, he noted with renewed approval the slim figure, golden-red hair, piercing green eyes that bored with equal impartiality into the soul of a person or the heart of the problem. The mole by her left eye—her only flaw—simply made her great beauty more striking. How old could Laura be? wondered Dr. Klein. Thirty? Thirty-one, maybe? Still unmarried, he knew. It didn't surprise him greatly. To use the old cliché, she was wedded to medicine, her first true love. There might be another some day in the future, but Dr. Klein doubted it.

"It's good to see you again, Doctor," Klein said, taking both her hands in his, brushing his thin lips briefly against her cheek. "You've had the last five days to yourself. Enjoy the little vacation?"

She smiled. "I slept parts of four of them. About three hours a night was my quota in the wake of that Kansas tornado. Bacteria, unfortunately, don't have unions. They operate on an around-the-clock basis. When the drinking water supply and the sewage systems get mixed up with one another, they work overtime. So do we. I guess we won. At least that's what my report says."

"I know. I just finished reading it. The usual, understated Messick prose. Except when you were describing the efforts of local medical officials. You sure heaped a bunch of coals on their heads."

"They deserved it, Dr. Klein. If things had been left to them, half the survivors still wouldn't have received innoculations. They seemed an incompetent bunch, and I said so."

"Congratulations, Doctor. I wish I had your conviction, your ability to evaluate everything in terms of black and white, with never a shade of gray in between. If possibly I had those attributes once, thirty years of battling the dragons of governmental Washington have slowed me down some. But that's neither here nor there. You've been a member of my department long enough to know I didn't call you down here to pat you on the head for a job well done in Kansas. That's past history now. It's the present that's bothersome, as usual."

"I would never have guessed, Dr. Klein," Laura said, all hint of a smile carefully hidden. The skinny Klein preferred to make his own humor.

"Well, when the day comes we've conquered all the diseases, you and I will be out of a job, won't we?" Dr. Klein said. He gave her a sharp look. Had she been mocking him? No matter. "There's an outbreak of bubonic plague in the Galveston, Texas area. Two deck hands off a Greek tanker anchored in the harbor went on shore leave and died three days later in a hospital. Other cases have been reported in Port Arthur, Texas City, and Rosenberg, so the two sailors must have infected others, and the circle is widening. I want you to take charge down there. How soon can you be ready to leave?"

Laura stared at him. "I haven't unpacked yet from Kansas," she said.

"Good girl. Dr. Finman will brief you on the specifics of the situation. The rest is up to you. Just get it stopped, and quickly. God knows how many will die before the radio and television stations can inform them that they may have been exposed to plague bacilli."

On her way to find Joe Finman, Chief of the Communicable Diseases Division of the Public Health Service, Laura Messick's green eyes were pensive.

Plague. The dreaded Black Death of medieval Europe that had decimated whole cities and countries, spread by infected rats and fleas and then by respiratory contact between human beings. But this, she assured herself, was the last quarter of the twentieth century. Man had invaded the moon and sent space probes to the outer reaches of the planetary system. Would he never completely overcome natural enemies from the animal and insect kingdoms infinitely smaller than himself?

February 6, 1977

"Sure is a pretty-looking piece, ain't it?" George Whitlock said.

"Yeah," replied Alonzo Cole, his mood as dark as the barrel of the U.S. Army issue M-16 combat rifle from which he was industriously wiping gobs of cosmoline preservative. "Peterson wasn't kidding about the weaponry. It's prime stuff. Just wish the rest of this damn lashup was half as good."

The two ex-GIs-turned-mercenary-soldiers shared a rare off-duty hour in their cramped tent, sweating profusely in the oppressive tropical heat, listening to the monotonous drip-drip-drip of the rain as it cascaded down on the canvas from the boughs of the jungle tree cover above.

"Aw, stop your bitchin,' man," Whitlock said. "What the hell did you expect, a picnic? You know what 'Nam was like, and we're making as much here in a week as we did in a month there. An army is an army. They're all the same."

"Only some more than others. We ain't had a minute's peace since we got here. Almost three weeks of bustin' our asses with chickenshit details. Chrissakes, we ain't rookies, we're professionals, we learned all that garbage years ago in basic. I'm tired of it already, man. Right off the top, the tents leak and the food ain't fit for pigs."

Whitlock admitted his buddy's irritable tirade was not entirely without foundation. Certain facets of Colonel Soames' operation were top-drawer, others woefully inadequate. Either the British renegade commander had deliberately chosen to ignore providing creature comforts for his troops, or had figured that for the salaries he was paying them they could simply go without, like it or lump it.

"And one more thing that's buggin' the shit out of me," Cole growled, taking a savage swipe at a large centipede crawling up his pants leg. "Peterson told me Soames was going to sell our services to the highest bidder. Who the hell's that? Ain't we got a right to know why we're here, where we're going, what enemy we'll be fightin' against?"

Whitlock lit a cigarette, idly watched the smoke drifting away into the semi-darkness. "Man, you do take on," he said. "You so all-fired anxious to stop a slug? And anyway, the pay's the same whether we wind up in Siberia or Siam."

Just then, the twin speakers of the camp PA system erupted into crackling, metallic sound.

"Attention, all personnel! Attention, all personnel! Muster in the mess hall at twenty hundred hours. Muster in the mess hall at twenty hundred hours. That is all."

Cole peered at his watch. 7:45 P.M. They had fifteen minutes before the meeting.

"Now what?" muttered Cole. "Always something. This outfit's worse 'n our old one."

"You know, Alonzo, if that old saying about a griping soldier being a happy one is true, you gotta be the most contented son of a bitch in Nicaragua! Well, let's go find out what The Man wants."

The mess tent leaked, like all the others, adding to the discomfort of the several hundred men gathered there. A blue pall from dozens of cigarettes, pipes, cigars hung in swirling tiers on the stifling air. Voices volleyed back and forth, a motley babble of tongues from half the nations of the world: English, Spanish, German, French, African dialects from Ibo to Ashanti, Swahili, singsong Oriental languages, Russian, Arabic.

The United States had its Peace Corps, Cole thought. Well, by Jesus, we're the War Corps!

The conversation dropped to an inaudible buzz, and finally ceased entirely as the stocky figure of Major Drobny, Soames's second-in-command, appeared, followed by the Colonel himself. Planting himself at the rear of what the troops derisively referred to as "the swill shack," Drobny drew himself up to his full height, arms at sides, and roared out, "Ten-HUT!" The massed ranks rose in unison, according the standard military courtesy due a commanding officer about to address them.

Leander Soames said, "At ease, men," spread his legs wide apart, locked his hands behind his back, and stared out at the sea of faces that comprised his private mercenary force.

The former British Army officer affected brush cut hair, a carefully clipped moustache, two grenades hanging from the web belt around his waist, and a holstered, pearl-handled .45 Colt revolver ("bastard must've seen George Scott in *Patton*," Cole had once snorted in disgust to Whitlock). When he spoke, his accent was pure Yorkshire.

"It has come to my attention, through various sources, that many of you believe you are being ill-used here, that your officers are hounding you unnecessarily, that information regarding our ultimate destination and mission is being deliberately withheld from you.

"Let me say the need for secrecy and security were prime factors in locating this camp so far from civilization. Officers and men alike eat the same provisions. While I admit the menu doesn't quite measure up to Claridge's in London, it's better than you have any right to expect in the jungle. I can do nothing about the rain or the heat or your general discomfort; after all you are professional soldiers, used to taking the good with the bad under trying conditions. I assume you will continue to cope.

"However, I do feel the time has come to reveal what the future holds for this troop. I owe you that.

"Through my contacts in the United States, word recently reached me that a Cuban Bay of Pigs veteran named Antonio García Belardo had set up offices in both Miami and New York to recruit fellow countrymen of his as mercenaries to fight in Africa. As you know probably, Fidel Castro's communist forces are operating alongside Soviet-backed rebels for control of the Alganam government. Best intelligence is they number about 7,500.

"I got in touch with Belardo and his group, which is called UNITA, the Spanish acronym for The National

Union for Total independence of Algana. They told me they wanted to obtain the services of as many Cubans and other Latins as possible, that they had literally hundreds of applications. Although Belardo was somewhat interested in my offer, it was apparent he wished to keep the UNITA involvement on a strictly ethnic basis—Cuban and Spanish-speaking volunteers only.

"He referred me to two other organizations. One was Alpha 66, a paramilitary force of anti-Communist Cuban expatriates, which claims a U.S. membership of 10,000 soldiers. They were not ready to make a definite commitment anywhere as yet.

"The other is known as El Kamas Enterprises. They are currently in the process of forming a brigade for duty in Algana. They were looking for specialists of all sorts, such as many of you are. Former Green Berets. Various technicians. Artillery people. Pilots. El Kamas suggested a union of their embryonic forces with mine, to bring their group up at least to battalion strength in the shortest possible time. I accepted, after having sounded out the black Marxist regime in Algana through a neutral third party. They have neither the money nor the desire to hire mercenaries. In addition, the Russian and Cuban aid is free to them.

"Since climate and terrain in Nicaragua are very similar to that of Algana, our training interlude here will be stepped up considerably in all phases of jungle warfare. I assure you we will take full advantage of the next few weeks, gentlemen. You will deem what has gone before a vacation. It is my intention to rendezvous secretly with the El Kamas forces at the port of Benguela, on the west coast of Angola, no later than March 15th.

"All units will be ready for intensive field exercises at 0600 hours tomorrow. Company commanders report to me in my quarters. That is all. Dismissed."

Later, lying in the soggy darkness, head resting on folded arms, nodding dreamily after his pre-bedtime fix, Cole mumbled, "Angola . . . so far . . . away. Africa . . . Chrissakes. How far's . . . that from here, George? Wonder what . . . women're like? Long time . . . since we got laid . . . huh, George?"

Whitlock chuckled. "Didn't anybody ever tell you guys on stuff ain't supposed to be interested in no foxy chicks? But then you always was a horny mother! Remember 'Nam, and those gook bar gals on Tu Do Street in Saigon? Sure wish we had a couple of 'em with us now! How the hell would I know what Angolan women are like? Same as any others, I s'pose. You'd better sleep fast, Alonzo. Oh-six hundred comes up mighty early."

Whitlock could have saved his voice. Cole was already snoring.

February 7, 1977

Transcript of a survivor's statement, taped by Panamanian medical authorities, following events that occurred 6 February at Ocochón (translated from the Spanish):

"My name is Antonio Gomez. I am thirty-three years old. I have a wife and ten children. No, let me correct myself. I *did have* before the bees came. It is still difficult for me to believe I am now a widower with seven children. I am the station master at Colón, at the other end of the Panama Railroad from our capital.

"Yesterday, a Sunday, was the feast day of my patron saint and namesake, St. Anthony. The priest in our village of Ocochón, Father Paredes, had organized a procession to celebrate the occasion. It started at the church and was supposed to arrive at the shrine of St. Anthony, a mile outside the village, for prayer and a special observance.

"The procession never arrived there. Instead, a beautiful religious occasion was turned into a nightmare I shall remember to my dying day.

"Sunday was unusually warm, even for this time of year, possibly more than a hundred degrees, although no one bothered to look at a thermometer. Everyone was sweating profusely. My five eldest sons, Juan, Emiliano, Luís, Paco, and Guillermo, all sing in the children's choir at the church. Father Paredes marched at the head of the procession, along with the Bishop. Next came men bearing the statues of the Blessed Virgin and Saint Anthony. After them walked the choir, including my sons. Other church dignitaries from as far away as fifty miles had come to be with us of Ocochón on this happy day. Last in line in the procession were the villagers, including my wife, Rosa, and our five other children, three girls and two boys.

"We passed the village plaza, the cantina, the hacienda of Señor Aguilar, the richest man in Ocochón, and neared the edge of the jungle. The uplifted voices were singing the praises of God and the saints. The children hopped and skipped along, trying to keep pace with the adults. They were eating candy and *dulces* as they walked, smiling and laughing. Of course, such things are forbidden by Father Paredes as being unseemly, but will God deny entrance into Heaven to little ones whose nature it is to be happy even amid a solemn occasion? I think not.

"Suddenly, with no warning, a child near the rear of the line gave a short cry, slapping at his face. He dropped the candy he was eating, and in an instant, his hands, sticky from the candy no doubt, were covered with huge orange and black bees, stinging, enraged, inflicting intense pain. Where the creatures came from, I know not. One minute the air above us was free of them, the next they were all over the place, in enormous clouds. Someone shouted to take cover, and the procession broke up. The candy and sugarcane eaters were attacked first; no one was later spared.

"Trying to protect our little baby, Elvira, my wife Rosa staggered a short distance, followed by a huge quantity of bees, enough of them to blot out the sun. Seeing that she could not outrun them, since she was again heavy with child, she lay down in the dust and wrapped her body around that of Elvira. Thus the young one lived, but Rosa did not. Seeing that she was literally black with bees—her face, her arms, her legs, all over—and screaming with terror and hurt, I tried to reach her. I could not, because I myself was set upon and stung a dozen or more times. It was like being branded with fire. I have never known such great pain, not even the time I was bitten by a poisonous snake.

"Meanwhile, at the front of the procession, although I did not realize it until later, Juan died protecting his small brother. He cradled him in his arms, ran like the wind with him to the fountain on the plaza, dumped him in, ordering Guillermo to stick his nose above water only when it was necessary to breathe, then slumped down dead. His body was found afterwards, swollen to twice its normal size from the bees' venom.

"Luís passed away early this morning in a nearby hospital, despite all the efforts of the doctors to save him. It was undoubtedly the will of God, Father Paredes told us, but I must confess it is a little difficult even for a man of faith such as myself to comprehend. Margarita was only five years old. Although stung just a few times, the Lord took her tiny soul also. Perhaps shock and fright caused her heart to stop, I don't know.

"In all, more than thirty persons perished. Dozens more are in hospitals. Some are not expected to live. Several villagers of Ocochón are blind due to bee stings in their eyes. But it seemed that the children suffered the worst of all, and the adults nearest them, because of the *dulce*s I suppose. The bees settled on them first, as I have recounted.

"Why does God send such plagues to torture those who try to observe his laws on earth. What is to become of me and my seven motherless children now? I am a simple man. I cannot see into the mind of God, so I cannot answer these questions. I grieve for Luís and Margarita and Juan and Rosa, may their souls rest in peace, and for all the families of Ocochón who lost loved ones as I did."

February 8, 1977

"By whatever yardstick you choose—the pseudo-scientific jargon of TV meteorologists, the Farmer's Almanac, the obvious discomfort of the daily THI, or the ludicrous thought of palm trees flourishing under the Golden Gateway Arch—our current weather predicament is beginning to border on the obscene.

"Although generally credited to Mark Twain, it was actually a late-nineteenth-century editor of the nation's oldest newspaper, the Hartford (Ct.) *Courant,* who coined the phrase, 'Everybody complains about the weather, but nobody does anything about it.'

"Apparently in the past few years, if not human agency directly then natural forces *have* done something about the weather. There has been no snow in Missouri since 1972, for instance. Winters have been abnormally mild in such former icicle-producers as Montana, Wyoming, Idaho, and the midwestern states. New England ski resort operators are going broke by the dozens. International Falls and Bemidji, both in Minnesota near the Canadian border, where temperatures this time of year could always be counted on to hark one back to the Ice Age, reported balmy weather in the mid-fifties yesterday, and we don't mean *below* zero, either. In Latin America, where it is now summer, record readings have popped thermometers from Mexico city to Tierra del Fuego. Our experts tell us much of the frenzied, erratic bee activity now rampant to the south can be attributed to the scorching climate.

"We don't pretend to know all the reasons, of course, nor do we think anyone else does. We can but cite various suppositions, all open to conflicting interpretations: Extensive nuclear bomb testing by the nations of the world that have disturbed and rearranged upper air patterns. Widespread defoliation of forest and jungle, due to high mercury levels and droughts, in turn causing unchecked, longrange passage of warm winds; heavy foliage is a prime factor in heat absorption. A gradual shifting of the Gulf Stream in a northerly direction. The theory that the earth is creeping closer to the sun. Secondary factors such as air pollution, aerosol sprays eating away the ozone layer of the atmosphere, something called 'the greenhouse effect.'

"Be that as it may, we earnestly long for a return to the good old days, when comedian Fred Allen made his famous weather forecast, 'Snow, followed by little boys on sleds.' It would be rather nice to see such a sight for a change, rather than getting up in the morning to go to work, peering out the window and wondering whether the heat had melted Busch Stadium during the night."

February 9, 1977

Fresh from their sack of Ocochón, agitated by continuing elevated temperatures into hyperhostility, their legions growing daily, the enormous swarm of bees rampaged northwestward toward the Panama Canal Zone.

The *adansonii* hybrids, while still in the minority, had begun to make their presence felt now, both in numbers and in genetic predominance. Tough and vicious, they took over hive after hive, hybridizing innocuous European bee cultures, terrorizing the bees which fell under their sway, fertilizing the queens of both strains with thousands of eggs daily. In Colombia, the ratio of killers to the total bee population had been somewhere, perhaps, on the order of one in a hundred thousand. It had now increased ten-fold, and soon would again.

While no one stayed around long enough to obtain an accurate count, estimates placed the bee swarms migrating up the Isthmus of Panama in the hundreds of millions, or even billions.

TEXT OF THE PROCLAMATION ISSUED BY THE PRESIDENT OF PANAMA:

"AT 8 A.M. THIS DATE, I DECLARE A STATE OF MARTIAL LAW EXISTS IN THE REPUBLIC OF PANAMA. ALL CONSTITUTIONAL GUARANTEES ARE SUSPENDED DURING THE GRAVE EMERGENCY CAUSED BY THE KILLER BEES. YOU ARE HEREBY ORDERED TO EVACUATE WEST OF THE CANAL ZONE IMMEDIATELY. TRANSPORT WILL BE PROVIDED FOR THOSE WHO HAVE NONE. LOOTERS WILL BE SHOT ON SIGHT. ALL WHO RESIST THIS ORDER WILL BE SHOT. OBEY OR DIE. SIGNED, ENRIQUE SORZA, PRESIDENT

February 11, 1977

In Tegucigalpa, the capital city of Honduras, a sixty-year old American named Henry Maddox drained a glass of rum, stared with bleary eyes at the denizens of the working-class bar known as La Zapatilla de Oro.

"Somebody sure as hell had a sense of humor," Maddox said aloud to no one in particular, banging the bottom of his glass on the stained bar for a refill. "Calling this dungheap 'The Golden Slipper!' Only gold around is in the proprietor's pocket, and the whores have a corner on the slipper market. Well, *a su salud,* Jose."

The bartender paid scant attention to Maddox. The drunken *Yanqui* had been coming in for months now. He was as much a part of the place as the furniture.

Mopping sweat from his brow, glaring with hatred at the slowly revolving ceiling fans that merely rearranged, rather than cooled, the hot, smoky air, Maddox reflected it hadn't always been this way, his being a sloppy bum with damn little present and no future whatsoever. Pride, arrogance, a stubborn inability to recognize a colleague's right of dissent, he admitted in a rare flash of genuine self-analysis, had all contributed to his current low estate.

"Selling mounted specimens of butterflies and giving English lessons to stay alive and keep myself in drinking money, for Christ's sakes!" Maddox fumed. "How the mighty have fallen!" What an abysmal comedown for a former leading light of the American scientific community, an entomologist of worldwide renown, author of three definitive books plus a slew of articles and papers on apiary activity, beekeeping, breeding!

No person had ever questioned Maddox's mental credentials or his grasp of subject matter. It was his hot temper, a tendency toward aloofness, and an overdeveloped sense of his own infallibility that created a vast gulf between Maddox and his contemporaries.

Even those unpleasant personal traits might have been written off as the eccentricity often accompanying genius' superior intellect, had Maddox not always stood ready to back up his theories with his fists.

Maddox remembered the black day when his life had begun to unravel. The date was etched in his mind with an acid-dipped stylus.

April 26, 1969.

Invited to present a paper on new findings he'd made through research into the alarm pheromones of bees, at the Annual Scientific Seminar in Philadelphia's Constitution Hall, Maddox had advanced confidently to the podium. He sneered at the smattering of polite applause greeting his appearance, then began to read. As he reached a critical and controversial juncture, he was interrupted by the sarcastic comments of Sverd Jensen of Sweden, a man whom Maddox had once publicly labeled a dangerous charlatan.

Angry words and heated invective led to an exchange of blows in the aisle, right in front of the Constitution Hall stage. Jensen fell heavily, striking his head against the wooden arms of a seat. Twelve hours later, he died of a skull fracture and massive subdural hemorrhage.

Charged by police and subsequently convicted of involuntary manslaughter, Maddox served four years in prison. Paroled and released, he dropped out of sight, wandering where his fancy took him until his random peregrinations brought him to Honduras.

Maddox was an embittered, alcoholic old man—true. Yet under the flab and the dirt he still retained a sharp and analytical mind. He probably knew more about bees than anyone else in the world. He kept abreast of the situation, read the literature, listened to radio and TV reports of the advance of the hideous killer bee masses, had even formulated certain theories he felt might, just might, be of value in repelling them. Cantankerously, however, he kept them locked tight within his head, not really giving a damn one way or the other, so long as they didn't menace him personally. In addition, Maddox had no real desire to aid an Establishment that had (as he viewed it) repudiated and exiled him.

On this particular night, intent on downing his rum, preoccupied with his private battle against unpleasant memory, Maddox failed to perceive for several minutes a stranger, seated to his immediate right at the bar. Then, suddenly, from a great distance it seemed, someone was addressing him.

"You talking to me?" Maddox asked, turning slowly. Blinking in the perpetual semidarkness of La Zapatilla de Oro, he picked up impressions of, rather than actually saw, the individual who had called him by name. American, obviously. Tall. Dark-haired. Wearing glasses. Studious, serious type, by his looks. A certain serenity in his eyes.

"I am. You *are* Henry Maddox, aren't you?"

"Guilty. So what?"

"I'm Roy Ramsdell, Maddox. To say I've had a difficult time locating you is the understatement of the year."

"Don't know why you bothered," said Maddox with a sneer. "It isn't going to do you any good. Whatever you're selling, I'm not buying."

Ramsdell appeared not to hear. "A few days ago, the President of the United States said to me, 'I need you. So does your country.' Now, I'm repeating the same words to you."

The light dawned on Maddox. "The bees! That's it, isn't it? You want me to help stop the bees."

"Right. The President has appointed me head of a scientific task force to find the answer. I can use a computer, analyze problems, usually come up with a solution on a long-range basis. About bees I know nothing. About bees you wrote the book. It's that simple. Every source I contacted in Washington agreed, grudgingly. Even though you wouldn't win any popularity contests to this day. I don't care. I want you on the team."

Maddox stared straight ahead. "Goddamn pack of stupid yoyos. Were seven years ago and undoubtedly still are. I'm not interested. Go peddle your papers and leave me alone." His stubbled jaw was firmly clenched.

"Mr. Maddox, your friendliness is exceeded only by your warmth and charm," Ramsdell said. "Anyway, I was warned in advance what your reaction would be. But this is a crisis, a real one. Speed is essential, so I'll lay it on the line to you. When you were released from prison, you hadn't served your full five years. You got out on parole. By leaving the jurisdiction, the state and the country without written permission from your parole officer, you were officially classified as a parole violator. The Commonwealth of Pennsylvania is prepared to press for your return. You have two choices, Maddox. One is working with me and my group, in which case all charges will be dropped. The other leads directly back to jail for a year or more."

Stubborn to the end, Maddox toyed with the idea of telling Ramsdell to go straight to hell.

Then he recalled the nearly fifteen hundred days and nights in the six-by-ten-foot cell. The stultifying work, for a man of his mental capabilities, in the prison laundry. The rotten food. His enforced association with the dregs of criminal society. No, he thought, going back to that was out of the question, given a viable alternative. Besides, if he were publicly adjudged successful in the campaign to cut short the depredations of the bees, he would be inflicting a stinging slap in the face to all his former colleagues collectively, which pleased Maddox mightily.

"You've got me by the balls, Ramsdell," said Maddox. "I accept your generous offer. But don't expect any great reformation in me, because there won't be any. When I'm right, and that's most of the time, I'll make the final decisions. I'll work independently, without any interference from you or anybody else. In addition, I'm getting along in years, I hate most people, and I hit the bottle too much."

Smiling, Ramsdell stuck out his hand. Maddox grasped it, without a great deal of enthusiasm. Despite the stains and smells of Maddox's filthy clothes, Ramsdell found himself almost admiring this crusty, aging iconoclast, whose fiery contempt and pugnacious spirit remained undiminished.

"Fair enough," Ramsdell said. "Just so we understand each other. Abraham Lincoln not only condoned U.S. Grant's alleged excessive drinking, he even offered to send a barrel of Grant's brand of booze to the rest of his generals. What's your favorite brand, Maddox?"

February 13, 1977

Kansas, thought Laura Messick, was a piece of cake compared to this Galveston mess.

Prior to the Public Health Service doctor's arrival in the port city, the outbreak of plague had followed a classic early pattern. The two seamen from the Greek tanker, already infected when they walked down the gangway of the vessel, later dying in a hospital ashore. The highly infectious and epidemic disease caused by *pasteurella pestis* organisms incorrectly diagnosed at first, its incidence in the twentieth century being so rare possibly one physician in a thousand had actually seen or treated a case. Confusion of the plague symptomatology—prostration, chills, fever—with a dozen other possible diseases. Positive identification of the bacterium through laboratory testing. Isolation and proper supportive treatment of newly infected victims. A crash program of widespread plague antitoxin innoculations. Finally, and most logistically difficult, the roundup of all persons suspected of having come in contact with established plague patients.

For perhaps the five-hundredth time, Dr. Messick asked the standard questions, took notes, crosschecked names, place, and dates against earlier depositions.

"You say you're a private pilot, Mr. Deal," Laura said, wearily brushing a strand of hair out of her eyes. "For whom?"

"Guy named Howard Hogson. Wealthy as Croesus, is the word. I've certainly no reason to doubt it. I know what he pays me, and the Executive Lear jet I fly him around in he laid cash on the barrelhead for."

"I see. It's also apparent you were in a Port Arthur restaurant called the Hellenic Feast, within the proper time sequence, having a meal served to you by the same waiter our investigation shows was exposed to the Greek sailors. You've received your innoculation, so you're safe enough. But when did you last see your employer?"

Deal did some figuring. "A week ago exactly, February 6th. I flew him to Japan."

"In other words, *before* you received your antitoxin."

"Yes."

"And Mr. Hogson hasn't been innoculated?"

"Not to my knowledge, no."

"Where does Mr. Hogson live?"

"In the goddamndest palace you ever saw, Doctor. Real posh Dallas suburb known as Highland Park."

Laura sighed. "The Big D," as most proud Texans referred to the city where President Kennedy was slain in 1963, lay three-hundred miles northwest of the Galveston-Port Arthur location. Trying desperately to contain the bubonic threat within a relatively confined perimeter, the last thing in the world she needed was a fresh outbreak in a place the size of Dallas. Hogson had to be found and immunized.

As she swabbed alcohol on Howard Hogson's massive forearm with a cotton square, it was obvious to Laura Messick that the multimillionaire Texan wasn't happy about her presence. He'd balked originally at Laura's insistent summons to Galveston, used abusive language, boasted of extensive connections in Washington circles, then abruptly caved in under threats of arrest and forced compliance with Doctor Messick's orders. Hogson was no fool. He was shrewd enough to admit she possessed the authority to make them stick.

"There," said Laura, laying aside her injection apparatus that resembled an open stapling gun. "It's all over, and you're still alive. What's more important, you won't get the plague. Was that so terrible?"

Hogson buttoned a custom-made fifty-dollar shirt. "Ain't the point," he growled. "Taking the time is what galls me more'n anything. Y'all have any idea what my time is worth? On the basis of my income tax returns, about a thousand dollars an hour. Plus I ain't used to being treated like some nobody by doctors, especially female doctors. I gave a hundred grand to two Dallas and Fort Worth hospitals last year, plus donating a kidney machine. When I walk into either of 'em, you should see the bastards bow and scrape. I tell you, money may not be the most important item in life, but it sure beats the hell out of whatever is second."

Hogson ignored, or chose not to notice, the savage expression of disgust that washed over Laura's face. In his own obnoxious way, he lived by the tenet that people without money, power, or both were hopelessly second-class, lower-echelon nothings placed on the earth for the express purpose of being exploited and discarded. It was also Hogson's firm belief that liberal infusions of cash could buy anything or anybody. Hadn't that fact been demonstrated over and over again during his twenty years in the Army?

A general officer in Korea and Viet Nam, Hogson had parlayed high rank, chaotic conditions, and a total lack of conscience into an enormous personal fortune. That his wealth was tainted by wheeling-dealing, black market operations, bribery, and, on a couple of occasions, outright murder didn't faze Hogson at all. To him, only the end result counted, and justified the means. Heroin, opium, penicillin, contraband war material, luxury foods, whiskey had all passed through Hogson's sticky fingers at one time or another as need and human misery fluctuated. On this very day, in dozens of warehouses in the United States and several foreign countries, Hogson had stockpiled a great store of goods in short supply, ready to move them on a moment's notice.

"Am I free to go now, Doctor?" Hogson inquired, pronouncing the last word with a pejorative nuance that made Laura see red.

"Yes, Mr. Hogson, you are," Laura said, her temper flaring. "Although I'd like nothing better than to prefer charges against you for obstructing a Public Health physician in the performance of official duties."

"Y'all could try, little girl, y'all could try," Hogson chuckled. "All this fuss because you happened to question my pilot. Hell, I've seen worse before, in the Far East and Korea and 'Nam, and I've always survived. Just about as big a deal as those damn bees I read about in the Dallas *Herald*. Over an inch long, stinging people to death, going to hit the Panama Canal any day, for Chrissake. Hogwash! Probably some kind of Commie plot, if the truth be known. I've more important things to do than worry about either germs *or* bees. Like supervising my interests all over the world, which I'm about to resume doing this very minute. Well, so long, Doc. I'll see y'all around some time, maybe." Hogson clapped a fawn-colored, two-hundred-dollar Stetson from Neiman-Marcus atop his balding head.

"Not very likely," Laura snapped. "Unless I find I have a legal case. Good day, Mr. Hogson."

Far to the west, in Los Angeles, California, a seedy, unkempt religious cult leader known to his flock as "The Prophet" (though he'd been baptized Gerard Evans Montague thirty years earlier) reached a decision he'd been contemplating for several weeks now.

Los Angeles was becoming too hot for him. Hence, the time might well be ripe to betake himself elsewhere.

Montague's pessimistic projections were unrelated to weather or climate. Instead, they were caused by the steadily increasing heat being generated by the Los Angeles Police Department, the growing suspicion on their part that "The Prophet's" activities could be construed as criminal even under the lax California statutes dealing with religious organizations.

There was, for instance, the once-trusting, tiresome Mrs. Burns, the little old lady with the big new bank account, courtesy of a recently deceased spouse. Of late, Mrs. Burns had begun to balk at Montague's oft-repeated, pious pronouncements that only those divesting themselves of their worldly goods stood a chance to enter The Good Place Above when the mournful hour arrived. It was only a matter of time, Montague calculated, before she blew the whistle and hollered "copper." Montague was extremely adept at reading potential danger signals in his marks.

And as if the Burns business wasn't bad enough, he had Esther to contend with. Esther Greenvale hid the mind of a three-year old in an overblown, provocative fifteen-year-old body. At their last meeting, she had steadfastly refused to terminate her pregnancy. Soon Esther's bulging middle would make this decision manifest to her parents, also members of Montague's "church," the California Disciples of Fundamentalist Thought.

No, before the whole lucrative gig fell apart, Montague told himself, and his considerable nest egg in the Valley Bank was discovered and impounded, a situation his arrest would certainly bring about, he would depart the smog-laden precincts of the City of Angels for a more salubrious climate. Its exact location was of small import to Montague, so long as an abundant supply of fresh suckers could be found.

Montague had, of course, read about and watched on TV news of the highly mobile, equally deadly, killer bees.

One night, he'd been struck with a sudden idea, hunch, intuition, or combination of all three.

Otherwise stable members of *homo sapiens* often did irrational things, panicked, when confronted by nature gone beserk, as in the case of the marauding bee swarms down in Central America. Suppose they came closer, which seemed likely, and actually entered the United States? Was it not reasonable to presume that a practiced con artist like Gerard Evans Montague could somehow utilize the advent of the bees to set up an "End of the world is in sight, give up your money before it's too late" scam?

It should be easy, decided "The Prophet," for someone of his undeniable talents.

Loading himself, his meager possessions, and the cash contents of his safe deposit box into a battered Volkwagen bus, he headed east out of L.A. toward the San Bernadino Freeway. Several hours later, he crossed the Colorado River Bridge at Blythe into Arizona. Breathing more easily, feeling a renewed sense of security, Montague allowed himself to make an obscene gesture into the rearview mirror toward the highway patrol vehicle parked on the California side.

February 15, 1977

Foraging through the deserted countryside, sending their scouts ranging in ever-widening sweeps to search out nectar-producing flora, occasionally venting frustrated rage on pigs and goats unfortunate enough to wander into their path, reproducing themselves at an alarming rate, growing daily more intractible in the steamy Panamanian Isthmus, the immense cloud of bees reached the town of Chimán, some 100 miles southeast of the Canal. There, in a display of senseless fury, they set upon and stung to death the only living creature they could discover—a harmless old cow, property of the departed mayor.

COMPLETE TEXT OF THE UNITED STATES' PRESIDENT'S STATEMENT ON U.S. PANAMA CANAL ZONE

CLOSURE POLICY, RELEASED TO PRESS, RADIO,
AND TV AT THE WHITE HOUSE BY SECRETARY OF
STATE ALLEN DELLMAN:

"As of midnight local time February 15th, I order
the Panama Canal closed until further notice to shipping of all nations. I take this step reluctantly, realizing the hardships it will cause to world commerce.
However, in light of the latest projections from my advisors, which place the bee swarm at or in the Canal
Zone within ten days, I am convinced to do otherwise
would be to act with total disregard for the lives of
ships' crews, American and foreign alike.

"The Panama Canal Act of 1912 very clearly vests
responsibility for protection of the Canal itself and the
entire Zone in the governor, who in turn is under my
supervision. Since in my opinion the current bee threat
falls within the Defense Against External Aggression
portion of that 1912 Act, I have placed General Westlake, Commander-in-Chief, Southern Command, in
overall military charge of Army, Navy, Air Force units
in the Canal Zone and immediate surrounding area.

"Civilian responsibility for combatting the seemingly
inexorable progress of the killer insects will remain in
the hands of Roy Ramsdell and his group. I have ordered General Westlake, as overall area commander,
to work in close liaison with Ramsdell, rendering
whatever assistance may be necessary.

"Since the start of construction in 1904, the United
States has spent roughly $6.5 billion building, de-
veloping, and improving the Panama Canal. It is to
safeguard this investment, possibly save lives, and allow the Ramsdell unit to work unimpeded in the vicinity that I have issued the order to shut the Canal for
its entire forty-mile length. As soon as conditions warrant, this order will be rescinded."

"That, gentlemen, is the verbatim text of the President's
message. We anticipate a flood of protest from all quarters,
naturally. Let me say I can sympathize with shipowners

for the additional cost in time, money, and inconvenience sending their vessels around Cape Horn will entail. To the President's words I can only add these of my own, blunt and harsh as they may sound. We are currently beset with perils our ancestors never dreamed of. We are forced into the posture of making hard and unpopular decisions in the interests of the United States as well as other countries. We make them unilaterally as they become necessary, and will continue to do so."

February 16, 1977

Inside a spacious repair shop belonging to the Panama Railroad, Roy Ramsdell and his mixed-bag staff of aides, which included both military and civilian scientists and specialists in various fields, toiled, sweated, figured, calculated, devised plans, tested them, made improvements, and in the end rejected 99 percent as unworkable.

Watching Henry Maddox supervise his section, Ramsdell thought the ex-convict bee expert had fitted in reasonably well with "Ramsdell's Irregulars" (as the media had soon come to dub the group), considering his past history and penchant for strife. While he still exhibited antisocial tendencies upon occasion and shouted in exasperation at subordinates whose knowledge and grasp of theoretical concepts were inferior to his own, Maddox's rehabilitation into something resembling a tolerant human was proceeding. At any rate, he was clean now. His shirt today was a brilliant white—almost blinding, in fact.

Ramsdell's strategy for delaying, stopping, or diverting the bee migration was divided into two general categories: immediate and long-range. He had placed Maddox in charge of the latter. Maddox had instituted programs embracing genetic experiments, possible dissemination of bee diseases such as American Foulbrood, and development of a kamikaze-type bee designed to suicidally attack its own kind. All had some merit, Ramsdell admitted, but also contained a major built-in flaw.

Their implementation could take months or years. The bees would be at the Canal Zone in ten days.

"Roy! Roy Ramsdell!"

Deeply immersed in thought, it wasn't until he heard his name shouted for the third time that Ramsdell focused his attention on Henry Maddox, standing before him, waving a paper in his hand. Sleeves rolled up in the blistering heat, perspiration plastering white hair in disorderly swirls against his forehead, Maddox's eyes gleamed with jubilation.

"Sorry, Henry, I was far, far away. What's up?"

"This. I've been out of touch with civilization so long I'd forgotten it. Norman Gary wrote it for the *American Bee Journal* back in '71, while I was in prison. Here, take a look. The paragraph I've underlined in red."

Ramsdell scanned quickly the indicated portion of an article entitled "Possible Approaches To Controlling the African Bee." Under the subhead "Mechanical Barriers," Professor Gary stated: At this time there does not appear to be a feasible mechanical barrier that might be used to stop the migration of the African bee. Theoretically, it should be possible to erect a "bee fence" that would halt migration at a given point. Migrating swarms probably do not fly very high above the ground. There is the possibility that a high, screen-wire fence, erected to lean 30–45° toward the bee-infested side, might function as a barrier to migration, if it were installed in somewhat open areas free of high vegetation. Control might be enhanced by placing trap hives beside and inside the fence. Such a mechanical barrier probably would not be feasible because of its expense and the necessity of developing other control measures in any event. However, the expense of permanently maintaining a bee-free barrier by other means is also rather prohibitive. Consequently, mechanical barriers should not be disregarded in our search for control measures. Any developmental research invested in this area may also have utility in confining honey bees to crop areas for pollination purposes. Recent technological advances suggest some strategies that might involve "electronic fences," utilizing beams of energy that repel bees.

Ramsdell nodded. "Goddamned interesting, Henry. But how useful I don't know, in this application. For instance, Gary says 'migrating swarms probably do not fly very high above the ground.' How would he explain the fact they surmounted the Andes when they spilled out of Colombia?"

"We're not sure they did, for a fact. There were no eyewitnesses, you know. The bees could have gone around or come through the lowest foothills, at night, just as well."

"Okay, granted. Let's even concede that Gary is right. I don't think by the farthest stretch of the imagination he ever envisioned the numbers of bees we're dealing with when he wrote his article. One more point, Henry. The terrain here at the Canal Zone. It's impossible. What the hell good would any kind of fence do around the Gaillard Cut, for instance? In that eight-mile section of the Canal that runs to Pedro Miguel Locks? You might as well try to stop an elephant with a peashooter."

Maddox scratched his chin. "I see what you mean. I guess I got carried away for a minute. Well, back to the drawing board. With any luck, I'll dig up. . . ."

"Wait, Henry. Don't jump to conclusions. Hear me out. We might just be able to modify Gary's ideas in some manner to fit our own purposes. Bees that lose their barbs in the act of stinging die right away, don't they?"

"Uh-uh. It's a popular misconception, Roy. When the barb is left behind in a person or animal, part of the bee's guts comes with it. Death ensues from several hours to a day or so later, depending on the severity of the injury to the bee's internal system. Trouble is, the damn things don't always leave the barbs behind in the victim, so they live to fly away and sting another day. The increased power and size of *adansonii,* we've proved conclusively, heightens the probability they can sting and remain undamaged. I strongly suspect that *adansonii* is immune to rules and regulations governing the stings of ordinary bees."

"But no matter what, some are bound to die, aren't they?"

"Of course, no question about it. But what are you driving at?"

"Remember the experiments your people conducted, goading bees into anger with electrically charged grids into stinging the grids, or at least a heavy plastic backing behind them?"

"Sure. We were doing some psychological reaction tests." Maddox frowned. "Only I don't see where that leads us. Gary suggests bee fences. You talk about electrification. There's no way, as you pointed out, of constructing an electrified fence the whole length of the Canal. For Christ's sake, Roy, it's forty miles from shore to shore, and fifty from deep water to deep water! And even if you perform the impossible, what guarantee do you have those miserable bees wouldn't simply wheel around the barricade, as they may have done at the Andes?"

"None," Ramsdell admitted. "There's something stirring around in my mind, the germ of a serviceable idea, yet I can't isolate it or make it take any tangible shape. Bee fence? No, not in the conventional sense as we understand it, *land-based*, that is. But, suppose we somehow, and this is where it's all unclear at the moment, *elevated an impediment suspended above the water near the shore farthest removed from the bees' advance?*"

Maddox considered. "I follow you for a while, then you lose me."

"Join the club, Henry. Let's go talk with Catlett and Barton. Maybe they can help clarify my thinking."

Major Pete Barton, U.S. Air Force, and Captain Eddie Catlett, U.S. Army Corps of Engineers, had been assigned as military liaison to "Ramsdell's Irregulars" by General Westlake in compliance with the President's directive. Ramsdell beckoned them over; the four men huddled around an outsized wall map of the Panama Canal Zone. The harried-looking scientific investigator briefed the officers on the essentials of his prior discussion with Maddox.

"As you will note," Ramsdell said, "I'm attempting to

combine Professor Gary's concept with the results Maddox's section obtained, but on a much larger scale. I have a hunch the end result should be something suspended in the air, quite high up, running the entire length of the Canal and even beyond, at or near the shore line to the southwest."

Barton stared morosely at the topographical rendering of the Canal Zone, as if trying to commit its features to memory. Suddenly, he snapped his fingers, spoke in a voice redolent of the red-clay country of Georgia, where he'd been born.

"The Air Force has been doing research for some time in the field of 'Instant Airstrips,' as they call them. Aluminum alloy, lightweight but strong as hell. Placed side by side, they allow fighters and bombers to land and take off before you'd have time to lay down a regular concrete runway. Navy Seabees installed 'em, or their distant ancestors, on places like Guadalcanal as far back as 1942. But the relatively crude stuff they used then wouldn't work now, what with greatly increased weight and take-off characteristics of modern jets. Anyway, they come in hundred-foot modules, with circular holes at six-inch intervals. Could be the answer, Roy."

"Can you get them airborne?" Ramsdell wanted to know, feeling rising excitement.

"Wouldn't be surprised, if we requisitioned enough helium barrage balloons, plus heavy-duty helicopters."

Ramsdell turned to Catlett. "How about electrification, Pete? A low-voltage charge of some kind, for instance."

"Hell, yes," Catlett said. "We have all the juice we need from the power substations that help run the various locks and gates of the Canal." He stabbed at the map with a forefinger. "Here, at Gatun Locks. Gatun Lake. Gamboa. Pedro Miguel. Two more at Miraflores Lake and Locks. The last at the Bay of Panama, on the Pacific side."

"Good enough, Pete," said Ramsdell, swinging back to Barton. "Where are these 'Instant Airstrips' being worked on, Eddie?"

"Wright-Patterson Air Force Base, outside Dayton, Ohio, last I heard."

"Check it out. As well as how many the Air Force can provide. I figure we'll need in the neighborhood of twenty-five, thirty thousand. Find out how long it'll take to send the strips to us on an A-1 priority basis. Coordinate your efforts with Pete, work out the logistics, report back to me in twelve hours. In the meantime, at my end, I'll ask General Westlake to hustle all the bodies he can round up in Southern Command here to the Canal Zone. We'll need a lot of help to install this whatchama-call-it."

Major and Captain sprinted away to start the wheels rolling. Maddox looked at Ramsdell with something akin to respect in his face, the first time he could ever remember so regarding another individual.

"It's a wild idea, Roy. The bee swarms fly into the electrically charged strips, attack and sting them. Mortality and confusion result, hopefully. Could just work out.

"Christ knows, there's enough scientific precedent in the literature. A few years ago, the USDA asked the National Academy of Sciences, your old outfit, Roy, to name a committee of bee experts to study *adansonii*. If I hadn't been behind bars at the time, I'd undoubtedly have been on it. Anyway, one of the committee members, Harald Esch of Notre Dame, experimented with provoking a hive of African hybrids, first with a gentle bump, then with a swinging piece of leather outside the hive entrance. Damn thing got stung ninety-two times in five seconds, if I recall the exact figures, and the enraged bees pursued Esch better than half a mile, trying to stick their barbs in *him*. Are you in the market for another suggestion?"

"That's what you're here for, isn't it?"

"Two points, actually. First, set the surface of the Canal afire with oil. The additional heat rising upward will enrage the bees that much further. Combined with the electricity, more of them should be goaded into stinging the barrier. Then, too, the smoke may tend to confuse the advance scouts until it's too late for them to warn the main body to avoid the trap. Second, in case the bees get any notions of flying above or around, equip some gunship choppers with flamethrowers. We ought to do some pretty dreadful execution that way."

Ramsdell grinned. "You know, Henry, every day that goes by I'm happier I rescued you from that sinkhole in Honduras."

"Maybe you are, but come to think of it, I'm not so sure about myself," said Maddox. "A man of my acknowledged reputation in the scientific community associated with a Rube Goldberg contraption like this. I'd be ashamed to have it become public knowledge."

If only for a few seconds, Ramsdell thought, Maddox had reverted to type; it would take a long time for the old leopard to completely change his spots. But now Ramsdell was going to steal twenty minutes for his meditation; it was the one personal activity he wouldn't put aside.

February 21, 1977

In the Nicaraguan jungle training camp of Colonel Leander Soames, matters were not going well for Alonzo Cole and his fellow recruits.

The British adventurer's mercenaries could count grievances by the score. Humid temperatures sapped them of their energy, left them weak and drained, ill-equipped to drill in endless military maneuvers. Officers and noncoms alike cursed and physically abused them almost without cessation. The constant rainfall brought yet another source of discomfort; wet uniforms and bedding produced a variety of festering sores that refused to heal. Perhaps worst of all, the ragtag army hadn't been paid, as promised, and the drug supply, described to Cole by Sergeant Peterson as "no problem", had proved far from regular. To a man, the troops were disillusioned, surly, on the edge of open revolt.

A North Korean officer named Kim Hee Pak furnished the spark.

Since before daylight they'd labored on tactical exercises. It was now past noon. Sergeant Peterson's unit, including both Cole and George Whitlock, had bungled assignments, botched weapons emplacements, stumbled in halfhearted, slovenly fashion through a simulated squad-strength fire fight all morning long. At length, thoroughly disgusted, Peterson called a halt. The lunch break was past due, anyhow, he thought.

Before the exhausted men could drop their weapons and sprawl on the ground, Lieutenant Pak came roaring up, shrieking in his native tongue, waving both arms.

Cole mopped his brow. "What's he saying, George? You got idea one?"

Whitlock said, "Shee-it, no, man. You know I don't dig that gook jive talk. And his English is almost as bad."

Pak shook an irate finger under the sergeant's nose. He was heard to translate, "Again, sah-zhent. Again. Make them do it again. And again. Until they get right. No eat. Not until they get right."

Whitlock protested. "Chrissake, Sarge, give us a break."

"Yeah," Cole chimed in sullenly. "We ain't doin' nothin' more until we have some chow."

Peterson shrugged. "What the hell can I do? He's wearing the bars."

Pak had heard the preliminary rumblings of mutiny. He strode over to plant himself before Cole and Whitlock.

"Very bad, black man, argue with orders of sah-zhent. Or officer. You be put on report to Colonel."

The fierce heat, his own tiredness, the idiocy of Pak's interference, the ethnic reference, above all the by-the-book injustice being committed against them, dissolved Cole's mind into a boiling maelstrom of fury.

"Who the hell you calling black, you yellow slant-eyed son of a bitch!" he shouted.

Lieutenant Pak grinned pleasurably. This was no longer a case for mere company-level military discipline. It had passed now into the realm of personal insult, to be settled in the casually bloodthirsty manner of the mercenary officer. With almost contemptuous slowness, Pak unbuttoned the flap of his pistol holster.

He failed to recognize the difference between Cole and

a frightened ROK peasant soldier, an error in judgment that cost him his life.

Since Pak patently intended to kill him on the spot, Cole moved to forestall him, reacting with decisive speed. Lifting the M-16 slung around his neck on a lanyard, Cole stitched a neat row of holes across Pak's midsection and watched his handiwork with admiring satisfaction as the lieutenant crumpled to the ground.

Hardly had the echoes of the two-second burst died away when Colonel Soames's command disintegrated into murderous warfare between enlisted men on one side, officers and non-coms on the other.

Peterson died in the first minute, nearly decapitated by a horizontal swipe of Whitlock's machete. Diving behind a rock formation that offered cover at the edge of the camp, Cole spotted the bearded, sadistic Captain Medina, formerly of the French Foreign Legion, a hated officer who had tormented Cole on more than one occasion. Continuous generalized firing had broken out everywhere by this time, the staccato sound of sidearms meshing with the rattling chatter of automatic weapons.

Cole yelled, "Hey, Medina! Over here! I'm gonna blow you away, you Spic prick! No more than you deserve, either."

The captain whirled, recognizing Cole's voice, snapped off several shots in his direction, pulled the trigger once more, found to his dismay he had an empty clip. With a startled look on his face, Medina cast aside the useless gun and sought safety in flight. Cole came out from behind the rocks, chased him, marveling that he could run at all after the assorted kinds of hell Peterson had put them through all morning.

Twenty yards ahead, Medina suddenly broke out of the jungle foliage into a small clearing. Off balance, stumbling, his vision partially obscured by the trees, Cole blasted wildly away at Medina. Missing the Spaniard, the slugs thudded instead into a hollow tree off to the right.

Instantly, a savage flock of wild bees, huge orange and black lightning bolts, zigzagged out of the rotting trunk searching for trouble. Medina ran directly into their path before he could put on the brakes. At the first sting, he loosed a frightful wail of terror that rose and fell, reached an unearthly upper register when the dark juggernaut covered his face, head, neck, and upper torso. For a moment, Medina's wildly flailing hands bought him a few seconds' more life. He was dead before he finally crashed onto the moldy vegetation of the jungle floor.

Alonzo Cole was more fortunate. Stung quickly into unconsciousness, he fell half-hidden beneath the fronds of a huge fern. Thus, when the battle of Soames's camp ended, with the officers slain or hiding, the mutinous rabble passed through the clearing on their way back to civilization. They paid scant attention to a pair of legs they stepped over en route.

Just another KIA, they thought, for the birds, beetles, and ants to gorge on.

February 23, 1977

It hadn't taken Gerard Montague, aka "The Prophet," very long to gather some new disciples on the road eastward.

His motley troop of assorted losers and malcontents numbered seven, including two sixteen-year-old girls running away from home, by the time "The Prophet" paused to regroup on the outskirts of El Paso.

Montague had followed with great interest press reports on the advance of the bees. He was aware, for instance, that they were nearing the Panama Canal Zone and that an egghead scientific type named Ramsdell had been spouting a lot of garbage about "massive government efforts" and "airborne defenses," or some such crap. Montague didn't really care, one way or the other. Actually, he hoped the marauding insects came a lot closer, because then for sure he'd dream up a foolproof method of tying his "Day of Judgment" con to the terror the bees seemed to be engendering in the population of Latin America.

"But what can I do here?" Montague murmured half to himself, fingering the jagged scar on the left side of his face even the beard couldn't completely hide, souvenir of a Berkeley police officer's billy club. "Too far away, that's what I am, too far away. I need to be closer to the action. People just ain't scared enough yet in the States."

"You still mooning around about them goddamn bees?" Anita Moore asked. She was one of the vagabond kids they'd picked up in New Mexico a few days previously. She was also, by Montague's lights, a dirty little slut who'd slept with all five men, and was probably making it with her girl friend too. "Why don't you and me roll a joint of that good Acapulco Gold you got, then go into the Volks and get it on?"

"That all you ever think of, sex?" growled "The Prophet," shoving her away. "There are more important things on *my* mind. Like how to make us some bread, for instance, before the whole L.A. bankroll is gone. Enough to keep us going 'til I can figure out a big enough scam the marks will go for, so we don't have to risk begging and stealing, maybe get ourselves jugged by these hick fuzz for nickles and dimes. So buzz off, Anita, willya?"

Reluctantly, the girl complied, spitting at him and hurling several vulgar names over her shoulder. Simultaneously, on the highway beside which the Volkswagen bus was parked, a late model sedan halted, discharged a passenger, sped on its way. "The Prophet" glanced up to note Ramón Villellas, the young, AWOL, Chicano GI who'd joined the caravan, charging toward him with ground-eating strides.

"Hey, Ramón, slow down, for Christ's sakes," said Montague. "What's happening, the pigs chasing you?"

"Not me, man," Villellas panted. "*You.* I hitched a ride into town."

Montague rose swiftly, poised as always for instant flight. "What the hell you talking about?"

"Your picture, man! I seen your picture up on the wall of the main El Paso Post Office, big as life! LAPD wants you for swindling *dinero* outta an old broad. And statutory rape on some chick. But that ain't all, man. The Feds are lookin' for you, too. A separate poster. Mail fraud. You're in a heap of trouble, man."

"The Prophet" groaned. A federal warrant. He put it all together. Those letters he'd incautiously written Emily Burns right after they'd met, that had to be the answer. Now the fat was in the fire, and sizzling. The Los Angeles hassles he felt he could handle. But the government people were another matter entirely—underpaid, tough, dedicated, tenacious. From them, experience had shown, there was no place to hide. On the spot, Montague abruptly switched plans.

"Saddle up, boys and girls," he yelled. "I've had a sudden revelation. Ramón carried it with him from El Paso. It tells me we should pay a visit to our neighbor to the South, where they have tortillas and tequila and rich American tourists. Let's put the show on the road."

Gerard Montague failed to add that Mexico was also blessed with notoriously venal police officials, who would easily succumb to a bribe if the need arose. Additionally, if the bees broke through the Panama defenses, sending refugees scurrying northward, the suckers might, just might, get the message. In that case, he, "The Prophet," who'd parlayed phony religion into a profitable living, was in business again.

The bearded con artist hummed happily as he started the Volks' engine. A few minutes earlier, he had expressed a desire to set up shop closer to where the action was taking place. With any luck, thanks to Ramón's sharp eyes, he'd be there sooner than expected.

February 25, 1977

EXCERPT FROM THE DIARY OF EDWIN CATLETT, CAPTAIN, U.S. ARMY CORPS OF ENGINEERS, 0396172 (set down several days later):

"It's fortunate I have nearly total recall. That, plus subsequent taped interviews with others on the scene, enables me to describe the amazing sequence of events with a fair degree of accuracy. So much happened in the space of little more than an hour on 25 February, above the Canal Zone, that's it's hard to know where to begin. First, perhaps a little recap of the past ten days might be in order.

"We're all exhausted. We worked nearly around the clock, setting up Ramsdell's 'bee screens' or 'bee fences' or whatever you want to call them. A part of our materials had to be landed at Panama City and brought to us by rail. The rest was air-dropped right at the site. I can report magnificent cooperation between the various military and civilian departments involved. SAC HQ in Omaha lent us all the Skymaster transports we could use. Anti-Aircraft Defense Command scrounged through every storage depot and warehouse in the country, and out of it, for the requisite number of barrage balloons, many of them no doubt World War II surplus. Wright-Patterson, Eglin, and Westover AFB's contributed mightily, as did several other Air Force installations. We had a whole slew of helicopters, both gunships and heavy-duty cargo carriers, manned by the most experienced pilots the Pentagon could round up. Most had served in Viet Nam.

"Our communications network was finally operative at about 2400 hours* of 24 February. We had a closed-circuit TV system connected with high points along the Canal, as well as direct radio links with all the helicopters. The railroad repair facility Ramsdell's bunch had requisitioned as a CP was reinforced with concrete and steel, as well as those thick, tinted glass windows that they use for spectators at nuclear bomb tests. Oh, we were perfectly safe, all right, which really makes me feel sort of bad, looking back on it, when so many brave men died out there in the line of duty. 'Killed in action,' the official reports and the telegrams sent to the next of kin will read. Well, I'll buy that.

* Midnight, military time.

They lost their lives trying to stop an enemy invasion. Whether that enemy was human or not, the end result wound up the same.

"Daybreak on 25 February was due at approximately 0530 hours. The rain was pouring down in buckets, the usual situation in Panama, one of the heaviest rainfall areas in the world. Outside temperatures stood at 108°. The electrified aluminum strips hung in place, the way Ramsdell had laid it out. The biggest anti-aircraft floodlights the Air Force uses lit up the scene, spaced at intervals down the whole length of the Canal. I can't guess how many thousands or millions of gallons of petroleum had been spilled onto the water. We waited for word of the bees' appearance, at which time Ramsdell would give the orders to set the oil on fire.

"At 0510, with just a hint of light showing in the east, the first radio report from one of the choppers came in. I'm paraphrasing these conversations; I probably don't remember every single word, but they'll be close enough.

"The speaker in the CP squawked. 'RI One, this is RI One-Niner. They're here. Over.'

"Ramsdell said, 'What's your position, One-Niner? Over.'

"'RI One, we're exactly midway in the Gaillard Cut, four miles from Gamboa, four miles from Pedro Miguel Locks. Over.'

"'What do you see, One-Niner? Over.'

"'I can only describe it literally, RI One, as a solid wall of bees. They're about a mile away, flying maybe fifty to seventy-five feet above the ground. Billions of 'em! They stretch farther than my line of vision, up over the horizon, for miles I'd guess. Over.'

"'Roger, One-Niner. I read you. Hold your position. Follow your instructions. RI One, over and out.'

"Ramsdell then gave the order to torch off the oil resting on the surface of the canal. It was relayed up and down the line to various personnel with flame-throwers on the ground, wearing heavy protective gear.

We saw the water come alive with flame. Thick, black smoke billowed into the air. I swear, this was a scene straight out of Dante's *Inferno,* what I can remember of it from college. The smoke, the heat, the rain, the bees, the hovering helicopters, the whole deal was incredible.

"But it must have been quite real to the bees, because they reacted almost immediately. Another chopper called in.

" 'RI One, this is RI Two-Seven. Over.'

" 'Report, Two-Seven. Over.'

" 'The bees are crossing now, from the opposite shore. They're starting into the smoke. They seem kind of—ah—confused. They should be at the metal strips in a few minutes. Over.'

"Henry Maddox said, 'Yes, yes, I'd counted on that. Their scouts, or guards, the bees that fly ahead of the main body almost like point men on military patrol, emit chemical alarms known as pheromones, substances such as isopentyl acetate and 2-heptanone, which warn of danger and mandate other bee activities. Smoke, such as we're employing, has a tendency to disguise or short-circuit pheromone emissions. Before they know it, the main body'll be in among the electrified strips.'

" 'RI Two-Seven, are you still there? Over.'

" 'Affirmative, R1 One. Something new now. Can you hear it? Over.'

"We all listened intently to the loudspeaker on the wall. What Two-Seven had meant soon became apparent. We'd gotten used to the racketing sound of the choppers' rotors in our ears when their pilots spoke, but by this time we were able to pick up another sound, gradually rising in volume, overriding even the noise of the engines. It was the steady, buzzing roar of the massed, closely packed bees, a thousand Niagara Falls rolled into one, a thunderous BZZZZZZZZZZZ-ZZZZ! BZZZZZZZZZZZZZZZZ! of hatred and frustration that curdled our blood. It was about now we could appreciate the wisdom of the President's having closed the Panama Canal to all shipping, despite the flack it brought down on his head. Also President Sorza's order evacuating the remainder of his people living west of the Canal Zone into Costa Rica. Vessels strewn over the length of the Canal and frightened civilians running about in terror would have been all we needed. God knows, the situation became grim enough as it was.

" 'RI One, this is RI Three-Four. Over.'

" 'Go ahead, Three-Four. Over.'

" 'It's tough to see, due to the smoke and rain, but the floodlights are helping some. It looks from here as if the main body of the bees is attacking the electrified grids. The strips are covered with dark bodies, swarming all over them. The air is thick with bees around my chopper, too, RI One. Lotsa flashes of light, both right and left. Those are the gunships, using their flamethrowers. They're cutting wide swaths through the bees, burning them up thousands at a crack. Even through my plexiglass, I can smell the result. Whew! What a stink! Three-Four, over and out.'

" 'We seem to be holding our own, at least for the moment,' Ramsdell said. Henry Maddox nodded.

"Right then, they seemed to be correct. As we reconstructed it later, the bees attacked in wave after futile wave against the barricade, coming in contact with the low-voltage electricity, stinging, dying. They perished by the hundreds of thousands, the millions, ultimately, but were replaced in turn by countless other hordes. The flamethrowers took their toll, too, as reports flew in from the various helicopters too thick and fast for me to record here.

"Although incalculable numbers of bees lost their lives, Ramsdell and Maddox congratulated themselves prematurely, as it turned out, for two reasons.

"There were too many of them. And they proved smart beyond belief.

"We got the first intimation a few minutes later.

" 'RI One, this is RI One-One. The bees seem to

have called off their attack on the barrier, One. They're gaining altitude. No matter how many we've been able to kill, more keep coming. There's just no end to 'em! I can see them settling on the barrage balloons in my sector now. The balloons are completely black with bees, as if they'd been painted on. I'm not sure, One, but my guess is they're stinging the barrage balloons. Hey, wait a minute! Two, no, make that three, balloons at map coordinates Charley-Seven and Fox-Three are becoming deflated, they're sinking slowly, faster, faster, the weight of the metal is dragging them down. They've just crashed into the Canal, I saw the splashes. Over.'

" 'Impossible,' I heard Maddox say, awe in his voice. 'Mass intellect. Almost uncanny ability to reason, to plan, to execute. Highly organized society, yes. Functions and class distinctions, yes, in ordinary *mellifera*. But never anything on this order. Why? How? I can only guess. These hybrids must have an additional ingredient besides size and aggressiveness. Apparently they have brains, too.'

"From that point in time on, the whole operation began to unravel. Everything went downhill.

"Barrage balloons were dropping right and left, their now useless burdens of electrified metal producing crackling flashes of eerie blue and purple light when they hit the water. In desperation, Ramsdell told me to cut the juice, it was being wasted. I did so. Our carefully set up defenses, which had looked so solid a few moments before, began to resemble straw fences in front of tanks.

"As if the loss of the barrage balloons and the barrier they'd been keeping airborne weren't bad enough, the damn bees added a new dimension in horror before they were done with us.

" 'RI One, this is One-Niner again. My plexiglass windows are totally covered with bees. They've cut off all vision. It's almost like they were acting in concert, doing it on purpose, I mean. I can see absolutely nothing. I'm maintaining altitude blind, by instruments only. These damn things won't let me go, One. My rotors must be killing them by the zillions, but it's doing no good. I . . .'

"We heard a grinding crash, the tinkle of shattering glass, then a despairing cry.

" 'What happened, One-Niner? You're above our TV camera range. Come in, One-Niner! Come in!'

"The pilot's last transmission was difficult to understand. 'Midair with . . . another chopper. Bees . . . all over inside . . . cockpit. Stinging me . . . blinded . . oh, my God . . no more control. . . .'

"The loudspeaker fell silent, except for the evil humming of the bees, which now had a triumphant note. A few seconds later, there came to our ears two separate and distinct 'SPLATS' as the wounded whirlybirds smashed into the still-burning waters of the Canal.

"Did I mention Dante's *Inferno* a while back? Not nearly a strong enough simile. The Italian poet's Hell was a state of mind, an abstract religious concept if you will, a matter one accepted on faith. This was different. Our Hell was right here on earth, we were experiencing it now, we were part of it.

"When the last casualty reports filtered in, we'd lost a dozen choppers and ten pilots. Only two were later rescued, more dead than alive, suffering from burns, smoke inhalation, and fractures.

"The mortality toll among the bees was fearful, from their stinging of the electrified airstrip modules and the barrage balloons, the action of the helicopter blades as they flew through them, and the flamethrowers. We discovered their bodies later on both shorelines of the Canal and covering the surface of the water like a crinkled, charred blanket. But it proved all in vain. Their numbers are enormous, in the billions Henry Maddox estimated, and it's likely we delayed their progress hardly at all.

"The whole terrible sixty-five minutes reminds me of a football game I played back in high school. We scored first on our opponents and knocked their star player out of action. We told ourselves we had it made, yet when the final gun went off, they'd licked us 43 to 7. At the end of that game, I felt the same way I do today. Sick at heart, hopes and aspirations crushed. And if those are my sentiments, being the relative spectator I was, can you imagine what it's like for Roy Ramsdell and Henry Maddox, the major architects of our defenses?"

The killer bees, their dispositions not sweetened by the countless dead they left behind them, passed over the Canal, fanned out through the western portion of Panama, and raged unchecked toward Costa Rica.

March 11, 1977

In the wake of the losing battle of the Panama Canal Zone, the extreme gravity of the situation could no longer be explained away by even the most optimistic. Newspaper, radio, and television provided the hard facts without embellishment. Unfortunately, these were augmented by the inaccurate tongue of rumor and word-of-mouth distortions more exaggerated with each retelling. The net result produced near-universal panic on the North American continent. The governments of Mexico and the remainder of Central America all prepared to declare martial law and evacuate the bulk of their populations northward to the United States. They felt that a nation with which they had long held commercial and geographic ties, a nation whose compassion for the downtrodden was epitomized in Emma Lazarus' famous "homeless, tempest-toss'd" verse on the Statue of Liberty, could not, would not desert them in their hour of need by refusing sanctuary to their citizens.

In this hope, as it happened, they were greatly mistaken.

The President made it very clear to Mexico and her sister governments that the United States was in no position to assimilate nearly 50,000,000 people *en masse*. No, the President said regretfully, it was impossible. Yes, he emphasized, refugees would be admitted, but on a selective quota system supervised by the Immigration Service.

When the President's words became known, feelings against Uncle Sam ran high south of the border. The old cries of *"Yanqui imperialismo,"* muted for decades, resounded once more from Mexico City to Rio de Janeiro. Wherever Americans living in those regions could be found, they were stoned, pelted with eggs and filth; embassies were burned, cars wrecked, the flag publicly urinated upon and dragged through muddy streets.

The United Nations hotly debated the issue, with no tangible result save for a fist fight between the United States U.N. ambassador and the Chief of Delegation from British Honduras, after which the session degenerated into a chaotic near-riot which New York police battled for hours before suppressing.

Meanwhile, as diplomats and politicians wasted their energies on interhemispheric squabbles, pointless oratory and a continuous spate of emotional appeals, the bees, unperturbed by it all, winged ever closer to the border between Panama and Costa Rica.

First a trickle, then a freshet, finally a surging floodtide of frightened humanity, the refugees flowed northward before them, bringing new sanitary, medical, health and food problems that soon overwhelmed authorities in areas where they halted.

In Washington, a haggard, drawn Roy Ramsdell, accompanied by Henry Maddox, reported directly to a joint meeting of the President and the Cabinet.

Their faces, Ramsdell thought, told the story much more graphically than any words might; reflected there were disillusionment, fear, the strain of trying to cope with the forces of nature gone beserk.

"Mr. President, gentlemen," said Ramsdell, "by now you are in possession of all the facts. I can add little to them, or make them any more palatable. They speak for themselves. We thought we had an excellent chance to stop the bees at the Canal Zone. For a while, we did. However, it was not to be. The attempt proved fruitless, with the result you know already."

"And now what, Ramsdell?" Secretary of Agriculture Jarvis asked bluntly, his huge jowls turned toward Ramsdell's grim face.

"In all candor, on the basis of our experience in Panama, there is nothing to stop the killer bees until they reach the Rio Grande River. And we have no certainty they can be contained at that point, either."

Ronald McKnight, boss of Health, Education and Welfare, raised his hand. "Can you suggest any new strategems that are being developed, or may be in the future?"

"No, sir, I cannot," Ramsdell replied. "Again, I would be less than frank if I told you to the contrary. Mr. Maddox and I and the rest of our team are racking our brains, night and day, to devise an effective and permanent method of halting the bees' encroachment. At the present, we have none."

His features as bleak as those of the rest of the group, the President intervened. "Where are you going now, Roy? Back to DeSales Street?"

"No, Mr. President. The space is too limited, and a Washington office is too far removed from what I believe will be the final battleground. I'm thinking of a field location. Perhaps 'command post' might be a better phrase."

"Do you have a specific place in mind?"

Ramsdell shook his head. "No, sir, except generally in the lower Texas area, somewhere close to Mexico and the Rio Grande River. It would have to be large, to accomodate my staff and equipment, both of which have grown since our BDI days. Of sound construction. And preferably underground, for obvious reasons."

"Hmmmm. I see," said the President. "Bill, could you be of any help?"

The Secretary of Defense, William J. Butler, rose. "I might, Mr. President, I just might." He addressed Ramsdell. "You realize we continually shift our ICBM sites around, to keep the Russians and the Chinese guessing, render it more difficult for them to pinpoint our weaponry in the event a retaliatory strike ever becomes necessary. There's an abandoned Nike installation, underground, concrete—the works. It so happens it's in Texas, between Alpine and the foothills of the Santiago Mountains. Ought to be ideal for your purposes, Mr. Ramsdell."

Ramsdell looked his appreciation. "Thank you. I'll fly down and look it over tomorrow, with your permission."

Other queries originated from the dozen or so men charged, through the constitutional authority of their departments, with responsibility for the lives and well-being of 220,000,000 Americans. Ramsdell, and occasionally Henry Maddox, fielded them with a mounting sense of failure, of futility. Both realized the Cabinet members, and especially the President, were shrewd and determined, not to be put off with evasions or taken in with false promises.

At length, Harvey Nettles, Secretary of the Treasury, said, "So far, this entire discussion has been predicated on the premise the bees are going to be obliging enough to attempt the crossing into the United States via the Rio Grande. There, in some mysterious fashion yet undisclosed, they may be stopped. Perhaps that is indeed possible, although we've heard no concrete evidence of it from either Mr. Ramsdell or Mr. Maddox. Now let me pose this hypothesis to you gentlemen. What if the bee swarm decides to fly in the opposite direction when the time comes? What then? Even if you can rig defenses of a sort along the river, how do you propose to handle the several hundred miles of land area contiguous to Mexico? By that I mean half of New Mexico, all of Arizona, plus Baja California, the whole damn distance from El Paso to San Diego in other words?"

Ramsdell opened his mouth to speak, but Maddox responded first. "A fair question, Mr. Nettles, for which we have no adequate answer at the moment. On the basis of the highly developed intelligence they displayed at the Canal Zone when they attacked the barrage balloons and helicopters, I'd say the bees were better than fifty-fifty bets to do just that."

"In which case," Ramsdell added quietly, "science wouldn't help a whole hell of a lot. We'd need a good, old-fashioned miracle."

March 15, 1977

MAJOR POLICY ADDRESS BY THE PRESIDENT OF THE UNITED STATES, CARRIED NATIONWIDE VIA THE THREE RADIO AND TELEVISION NETWORKS AND TO FOREIGN COUNTRIES BY COMMUNICATIONS SATELLITE:

"Good evening, my fellow Americans. I stand before you tonight to clarify my position, and that of the Congress, on several matters that have recently come to the forefront since the menace of the bee migrations began several months ago.

"There is no doubt whatsoever that, while it may seem currently remote to United States citizens, the very real possibility remains that all of our lives may be affected in the not too distant future.

"In any event, to natives of other lands, the future is now, this very minute. In Mexico, in Guatamala, in the rest of Central America, fugitives are fleeing from the onrushing killer bees as medieval Europeans once did from the deadly spread of the Black Death. Governments have clamored, amid this crisis, for us to admit their refugees without restriction into the United States. Our refusal to do so has been met by scorn, insults, condemnation, and even bodily harm to Americans dwelling in those countries.

"I have no doubt many listening to my voice thought that the United States' tradition of lending assistance would win out in this instance over the better judgment of legislative, judicial, and executive branches of your government. To those, I state categorically it has not. That tradition must be regretfully shunted aside, in favor of the exigencies of national interest. Acting otherwise would be to repudiate every word contained in the oath of office I took fourteen months ago.

"Therefore, the Immigration Quota System will remain in effect until further notice. Despite the 'One Worlders' and 'turn-the-other-cheek' advocates who would extend the hand of friendship to mobs who sully our flag and shout at our people 'Go Home!' the realities of 1977 mandate at least a partial return to a policy of isolation, and America first for Americans. If that seems heartless, selfish, and against the principles our forefathers fought for, it cannot be helped.

"I exhort all of you to go about your daily work and living as before. Do not, I beg of you, panic. Do not look to your leaders to declare martial law, as has been done in several countries already in the path of the oncoming bees, or to suspend constitutional guarantees. All civil liberties ordinarily enjoyed by our citizens will remain in force, with one exception. Let me explain more fully.

"Due to the extreme dangers involved, on both domestic and foreign levels, no civilians will be permitted to enter Mexico or Central America until further notice. Train, plane, and steamship travel to those regions is expressly prohibited until further notice. I have ordered the Treasury Department, Immigration Service, Bureau of Narcotics and other appropriate agencies to augment their personnel patrolling our common borders with Mexico. This also is in the interest of national security, but, beyond that, to protect American lives.

"I have issued orders, additionally, that Americans residing in the aforementioned nations be evacuated as soon as practicable, including diplomatic, cultural and scientific staffs, members of the Peace Corps, and the like.

"Finally, let me state that our best minds, and I assure you we have tapped every available source, are hard at work to abort the bee problem before it can take the life of a single person living within the confines of the continental United States. Unhappily, American fatalities have already resulted directly from the unprecedented activities of the huge bee masses in Colombia, Panama, and the Canal Zone. I pledge to you my sacred honor it will not happen here.

"Thank you, and good night, my fellow Americans."

April 6, 1977

At a somewhat more leisurely pace than their former steady, ten-mile-a-day clip, the battered bees proceeded on a northwesterly course up the coast of Costa Rica toward the city of Limón, whose inhabitants promptly abandoned it for the duration. However, for no apparent reason, they then swung inland and halted on the broad, lush plain between Vesta and Perjivalle.

April 7, 1977

EXCERPT FROM *EL DIARIO DE SAN JOSE*, LEADING DAILY NEWSPAPER OF THE COSTA RICAN CAPITAL (TRANSLATION FROM THE SPANISH):

By Julio Vargas

San José, April 7—"Latest communiques from the bee front indicate astounding and heartening developments are taking place. The insects have stopped in a gigantic encampment, contained in a circle estimated at ten miles in diameter, about sixty miles from our city. Aerial reconnaissance reports from the Costa Rican Air Force state the bees are seemingly content to remain in the same area, as they have for the past several days. One observer said: "They remain motionless on everything in sight on the ground—trees, buildings, rock formations, scrub growth—as if a permanent part of the landscape. It is as though they are resting, pondering their next move, if any.'

"News reaching here from the United States and from Panama, concerning the efforts of Roy Ramsdell, head of a technical group assigned the task of neutralizing the bees, indicated Ramsdell's evaluation of the damage inflicted on the bee migration at the Canal Zone was summed up by the word 'negligible.'

"However, the fact the bees have ceased moving may mean he was in error, that in actuality they were badly mauled by the 'bee screens,' flamethrowers, and other stumbling blocks Ramsdell threw in their path.

"If this assumption proves correct, then the possibility exists that their current bivouac will be the prelude to a retreat southeastward, whence they originated.

"Most knowledgeable bee men believe, on the other hand, it is merely the lull before the next storm. Which theory is correct, time alone will tell.'

April 9, 1977

Though terribly weak and shaky, he was indisputably alive, thought Alonzo Cole, cowering behind a heap of bomb-blasted rubble on the Avenida Roosevelt, the broad main boulevard of Managua. How much longer he would remain so was anybody's guess, considering the fullscale war he'd stumbled into in Nicaragua's capital.

Face and arms swollen from the venom the bees had left in his body, Cole had returned to consciousness a vastly surprised individual. Discovered by two *zambos,* native Nicaraguans of mixed Negro and Indian blood, on their way to market in an ox cart, Cole had been dragged from the scene of the massacre at Soames's camp to their village. There, with the assistance of herbs, native medicines, chanted incantations, and a great deal of luck, the *zambos* nursed back to health the young American who partially shared their racial background. Through sign language and the minimal communication Cole and his benefactors were able to effect, between his poor Spanish and their unfathomable dialect, Cole gathered he had lain out of his head for the better part of a week.

A further by-product soon became manifest. For the first time he could remember since 'Nam, Cole found himself detoxified, free from drug addiction. Apparently he had kicked, gone cold turkey during the lost, delirious seven-day period that remained a total blank in his mind. It was, he reflected, the *only* way he could have done it.

Walking mostly, riding when he could, begging or stealing food, Cole had finally arrived in Managua to seek the help of the American consulate in obtaining passage back to the States. New York City held few attractions, true; Nicaragua, since Colonel Soames's private army had evaporated, none at all.

Too late, Cole had realized he could solicit no aid from the diplomatic people; he had no passport, was in the country illegally, might even be connected with some of the deaths at the training camp. But in any event, the whole question turned out to be academic. The American Consulate had ceased to exist. The building stood empty, windows smashed, walls disfigured with scurrilous Spanish graffiti, its staff evacuated, dead, or scattered.

"Those bees! Those motherfucking bees! They're the cause of all this, goddam them! First the people riot, then a bunch of Army officers grabs the opportunity to start a civil war and put themselves into power." Cole was talking to himself, and having difficulty hearing his own words. Aircraft swooped overhead. Bombs and mortar rounds kept dropping in the vicinity. Small-arms and automatic-weapons fire added their contribution to the overall bedlam.

Cole was right, of course. The bees had started it. Panic. Martial law. Citizens trying to escape, in all directions, and by any means of transport. Finally, rebel forces battling Managuan police and regular troops.

Rail communications with Corinto and Granada, respectively ninety and thirty miles away, were severed. The mass exodus had choked the Pan-American Highway with pedestrian traffic and cars. Men had been murdered for the vehicles they were driving. A pall of smoke wreathed the once-beautiful city, stemming from a score of fires, obscuring the crater lakes of Asososca and Nejapa in the newer, more affluent residential sections, and Tiscapa, behind the Presidential Palace. That structure lay under heavy siege to the south. Vandals had destroyed the monument to Nicaragua's most famous poet, Rubén Darío, in the Parque Darío at the northward extremity of Avenida Roosevelt. Shells had damaged both the National Palace and Managua's modern, twentieth-century cathedral. Fatalities could be numbered in the hundreds. No one had yet bothered to count the wounded and injured. The rebels had seized radio stations, telephone exchanges, power plants, hospitals.

Claim and counterclaim. Advance and retreat. Looting, arson, theft, vandalism, assassination. Rumors flew thick as flights of arrows in Managua, compounding the confusion.

A piercing whistle, followed by an ominous "CRUMP-CRUMP" sound, signaled the advent of incoming mortar rounds not far from Cole's position. Dust and small stone fragments sprayed over him.

Oblivious to the danger, disgusted, fed up, nerves frayed by the bombardment and his own tenuous situation, Alonzo Cole leaped up, shook his fist at the unseen weapons firing in his direction.

"Goddamn you, you miserable bastards," he howled. "Stop shooting at me! I've had a bellyful of war and killing and dead bodies. All I want now is to get home in one piece. Can't you see that? Is it asking so much?"

Inexplicably, for the first and only time in his life so far as he could recall, Cole sank to his knees, began weeping uncontrollably with great suddering sobs. Unheeded, his tears mingled with the dirt of a ruined street in a foreign city he feared might become his grave.

April 11, 1977

El Diario's cautious optimism proved myth, delusion, a castle of hope built on quicksand, false as a mine salted with Fool's Gold.

The bees had started to move again.

The President of Costa Rica, Adolfo Vallejo, acted promptly. He ordered reserve military units to duty, evacuation of government heads to Puntarenas (fifty miles west on the Gulf of Nicoya), and implementation of a long-discussed contingency plan, "Operation Scorched Earth."

April 11, 1977 (later)

EXCERPT FROM A BROADCAST, HEARD THROUGHOUT THE UNITED STATES ON MEMBER STATIONS ORIGINATING FROM NBC RADIO NEWS AND INFORMATION SERVICES, NEW YORK:

ANCHOR: "The top story of the hour . . . gigantic swarms of bees, last reported stationary for several days in central Costa Rica, now airborne and winging their way toward San José, the capital. Costa Rican officials have instituted certain new control measures, as we hear now from NBC Radio News Correspondent Emerson Thornton, in San José.

THORNTON: " 'Operation Scorched Earth' began at daybreak today on an almost countrywide scale. In a last-ditch attempt to deny the bees any food sources, thereby forcing them to backtrack, President Vallejo has instructed that all crops throughout Costa Rica be destroyed or rendered inedible by fire, dynamite, or toxic chemicals.

"Since *apis mellifera adansonii*, the Africanized Brazilian bee, is known to be resistent to DDT, Costa Rican agricultural experts are employing a variety of other pesticides. Results will be announced within a short time. President Vallejo said today jungle and forest, coffee and cocoa crops, banana plantations, corn fields, literally everything that grows and can be even remotely considered a source of nectar, will be sprayed with such lethal compounds as methyl parathion, aldrin, dieldin, EPN, heptachlor, and propoxon.

"When queried by this reporter concerning the long-range effects of the crop destruction on the economy and population of Costa Rica, as well as the harmful properties of the pesticides on human beings, President Vallejo said, and we quote, 'If we cannot conquer the bees by these methods, there will be no people left in Costa Rica anyhow.'

"Emerson Thornton, NBC Radio News, San José."

April 18, 1977

HAM RADIO TRANSMISSION MONITORED BY UNITED STATES LISTENERS, AMONG MANY OTHERS, ON THE 20-METER BAND:

"CQ Emergency! CQ Emergency! This is Tango India Two Kilowatt Golf Alpha, outside Cuidad Quesada, Costa Rica. My name is Timmy Benjamin. I'm thirteen years old.

"An unbelievably huge cloud of bees is attacking the plantation my father managed for the Flagler Coffee Company. I'm using the past tense, because I'm sure my father's dead, and my mother too."

"I'm broadcasting from a special concrete bunker with heavy screens over the window Dad built for our protection. Some of the plantation workers who stayed behind made it to safety here with me, but the rest . . . they . . .

"From where I'm sitting, I can see Mom and Dad, lying halfway between the house and the bunker. There are bees all over them. One bunch rises, and then another dives in, stinging, wild, as if they'd gone crazy. I guess it must be hunger more than anything, and the heat too, not only from the weather but from the fires the Costa Rican government set to burn the crops.

"The bees attacked early, without warning almost. I was within a couple of steps of the bunker. I'd brought my ham radio set here after Dad built the bunker. I heard what sounded like a murmur at first, then it grew louder, until it sounded like a whole lot of airplanes being revved up at once. They streamed in over the treetops, through the smoke, a black column that blotted out the sky. I couldn't begin to estimate the numbers.

"I shouted to Mom and Dad to either get back in the house or run here, but it was too late. What I saw the bees do . . . was . . . horrible . . .

"Right now, I don't know how many big, furry bees are beating against the window screens, trying to get in. Quick as I moved, I was stung a couple of times before I could close the bunker door.

"Lots of our workers are dead. José Pintero, the foreman, tried to lead Mom to safety, but he was killed. It's not just the insane way the bees are acting. But the size! I swear, a few of them look like they're two inches long! Really 'superbees!'

"What has happened here is a tragedy in more ways than one, because it could have been avoided. With tears in his eyes, Dad told José to have everything burnt, as President Vallejo requested. Then the soldiers and the Ministry of Agriculture came and sprayed a lot of poison stuff over what was left.

"But somebody, in all the confusion, forgot to destroy, or at least move underground, a shipment of sugar that just arrived from San José. I can see the bees crawling all over the sacks, late arrivals dropping down on top of the ones already there, trying to reach the sugar. More are joining in all the time. I can't even see the house now for the bees. They're flying around like they're crazy, going to the burnt-out coffee plants, then back to the sugar sacks. . . .

"There's gotta be millions of them! We have food and water in the bunker. But who can tell how long they'll stay around the sugar? I don't know if we can last . . . Somebody, please, if you hear me, send help . . ."

At least three of Timmy Benjamin's listeners, ham enthusiasts located in Hawaii, Wisconsin, and Ohio, recorded his heart-rending transmission on tape. The news leaked out, reporters called, eventually verbatim transcripts appeared in the Honolulu *Advertiser,* Milwaukee *Star-Journal,* and Toledo *Blade.* UPI and AP picked the story up, feeding it to their legions of radio and newspaper wire subscribers. In short order, the American public heard and read for the first time an eyewitness account of an attack by killer bees while actually in progress.

They remembered the President's recent speech. They wondered. They grew fearful. At length, on the basis of Timmy Benjamin's short, powerfully graphic description, one inescapable conclusion emerged.

Despite the President's ringing assurances, it *could* happen here.

April 19, 1977

STATEMENT MADE BY PRESIDENT ADOLFO VALLEJO FROM THE TEMPORARY SEAT OF THE COSTA RICAN GOVERNMENT AT PUNTARENAS (IN ENGLISH AND SPANISH):

" 'Operation Scorched Earth' must now be officially considered a failure. Notwithstanding the intense efforts of our military and governmental personnel and massive destruction of crops plus use of pesticides known lethal to bees, no noticeable results have been achieved.

"Many bees are dead from ingestion of various poisons. Their corpses litter the ground of our country by the millions. But billions more fly unchecked through the skies above us. The way lies open to our fellow Latin American nations, Mexico, and ultimately the United States, unless intelligences far superior to ours can bar this unspeakable migration that threatens the peace and sanity of the entire Western Hemisphere.

"I am unable to find comforting words. There are none. Clearly, our strategy of cutting the bees off from food supplies did little or no good, delayed their relentless timetable for but a short period. As an unhappy by-product, it heightened their already hostile and aggressive natures, for many attacks on people and animals have been documented since 'Operation Scorched Earth' began eight days ago. American and Costa Rican lives were lost yesterday near Cuidad Quesada. Undoubtedly, others will be.

"At this point, my only advice to my countrymen must be: save yourselves if you can. Go with God."

April 20, 1977

If the President calculated that his televised policy address of March 15 would serve to unify the country, weld dissident philosophical elements into a "rally-round-the-flag" posture, his normal political acumen failed him badly.

Seeing eye to eye with one's neighbor down the street on such controversial subjects as religion, the conduct of government, sports, ethnic considerations, sex education, abortion, welfare, or the expenditure of tax dollars had never been a noticeable national trait. For too long rugged individualism and the Constitution-protected right of disagreement had been engraved on the American ethos. Even World War II, marked by nearly total unanimity of purpose among United States citizenry to resist external aggression, still produced its share of "antis," dissenters, collaborators, objectors, downright traitors.

What history books will one day designate "The Great Refugee Debate" proved no exception.

The ban on travel to the South, due to the peril of the rampaging bees, had been shrugged off as a necessary evil. The President's firm stand against admission of millions of refugees, however, and the Congressional approval that backed it, became an explosive issue that divided America within days into two hostile camps.

One, "The U.S. For Us," composed largely of conservative elements, supported the Chief Executive, advocated isolation, and tough adherence to immigration quotas. The other, "Admit The Refugees Now!"—its ranks swollen by liberal-leaning thinkers—contended that the only humanitarian course was to open the gates wide to unlimited numbers of bee-displaced persons, turn the country into a huge Ellis Island.

Letters pro and con poured into Washington, addressed to the President, the 435 Congressmen and 100 Senators, in such enormous volume that the entire postal system almost ground to a halt. Night and day saw demonstrations, torchlight parades, televised debates, impassioned speech-making, in some cases bloody pitched battles between adherents of the two conflicting groups.

Always eager to discomfit the United States, third world nations, allied with the Communist bloc, forced reconsideration of the whole thorny problem in the Security Council. Its consensus was to admit the refugees. A U.S. veto effectively stymied the UN move, but did nothing to deal with the root cause.

Acting on a petition for injunctive relief sought by the national "Admit The Refugees Now!" organization, a Federal Court judge with liberal leanings and an elastic interpretation of statute issued a blanket writ against the President and the Congress, requiring them to show cause why the millions of Mexican and Latin American refugees should not be allowed to enter the United States. Immediately, the Attorney General cried "Foul!," proclaiming the procedure without legal precedent as well as patently unconstitutional. He then filed a brief with the Appellate Division, requesting a reversal, in the full knowledge that, whatever the decision ultimately handed down, the whole sorry mess would be finally bucked up to the Supreme Court.

April 23-25, 1977

During a forty-eight-hour period in late April, newspaper headlines apprised their readers of the power of pressure, when translated into numbers, to change lawmakers' minds:

CONGRESS REVERSES STAND, WILL ADMIT REFUGEES —*San Francisco Chronicle.*

PRESIDENT CITES PUBLIC OPINION LEVER IN REFUGEE CRISIS—*Los Angeles Times.*

NATIONAL UNITY OUTWEIGHS NATIONAL SECURITY IN REFUGEE ISSUE, SAYS PRESIDENT—*Portland Oregonian.*

HOUSE DIVIDED MUST FALL, PRESIDENT TELLS US; OPENS DOORS TO REFUGEES—*Houston Post.*

PRESIDENT NIXES POSSIBLE VETO OF REFUGEE ADMISSION BILL—*Chicago Tribune.*

PRESIDENT ASKS TOLERANCE OF NATION, FORESEES TROUBLE IN WAKE OF REFUGEE ADMISSION—*Des Moines Register.*

PRESIDENT PROPOSES MAN-MADE 'DP CITIES' TO HOUSE LATIN-AMERICAN HOMELESS—*St. Louis Post-Dispatch.*

CAMPS TO BE LOCATED IN SOUTHWEST AND WEST—
Hartford Courant.

TEX., N.M., ARIZ. NAMED 'DP' STATES—*New York
Daily News*.

NEVADA, WYOMING, MONTANA TO ACCEPT REFUGEE
SHARE—*Boston Globe*.

April 26, 1977

Night and day had ceased to exist in the former Nike
missile installation buried beneath the baking plain of
western Texas. Ordinary time demarcations vanished, became merely a blur as clock hands raced in a surreal
rigadoon toward Doomsday.

Every member of "Ramsdell's Irregulars" existed on
minimal sleep, hastily snatched meals, black coffee—and
hope.

Hope that the voluminous input fed into the multiple
computer banks would result in some startlingly informa-
tive feedback. Hope that hundreds of years of combined
knowledge, experience, and experitise could somehow
fashion a foolproof barrier against the invader bees. Hope
that one, or both, of these much-desired outcomes sur-
faced before their deadline had come and gone.

Busily engaged in surpervising a unit about to insert
new programming modules into the sophisticated COBOL
system, Roy Ramsdell wondered why he felt so dizzy all
of a sudden. He put a hand to his head and was surprised
to discover his forehead drenched with perspiration.

"Shouldn't be," he muttered thickly, "air conditioning's
on in here."

When the dizziness abated a trifle, other more alarming
symptoms appeared. Ramsdell's stomach began to churn
and heave. He ran to the nearest lavatory, barely making
it inside before losing his lunch. Ramsdell swayed, nearly
blacked out entirely, and sat down hard on the floor. Af-

ter a while, from a great distance, he realized someone was pounding on the door. It drained the last of his strength to reach up and unlock it. Henry Maddox's solicitous face peered down at him.

"Hey, Roy, you okay?" Maddox wanted to know. "I saw you make a beeline for the john. That's not the best choice of phrases around here, come to think of it, but it's an apt description. Anyway, I heard you vomiting. What gives?"

Ramsdell shook his head. "I dunno. I just feel rotten. Ache all over. Sore throat. Dizzy. Sweating. Fever. Some kind of bug, I guess. I'll be all right."

Maddox snorted, "In a pig's ass you will. From all external appearances, you'll be dead before morning if you keep walking upright and trying to function. To say nothing of giving whatever it is you have to all of us. That we can't afford. But first things first. Get into bed and stay there. Leave the rest to me."

Nothing loath, Ramsdell allowed Maddox to lead him into the tiny cubicle he called his living quarters. Lying flat on his back, Ramsdell thought, didn't seem to improve matters much.

On the dead run, Maddox crashed headlong into Barney Lippert, Ramsdell's second-in-command back at the Washington "think tank," a whiz with the computers and almost everything else.

"What's up, Maddox?" Lippert inquired. "Damn place on fire?"

"Worse than that. Roy's come down with what appears to be a virus. He's sick as hell. I think a doctor should see him. You have any idea where I can latch onto one willing to make a house call at a Nike missile site?"

"Well, I heard on the grapevine there's a Public Health Service M.D. over in Alpine, just arrived last night. Washington sent her to set up sanitary and health arrangements in the refugee city they're throwing together near here. Name's Messick, Laura Messick. You might try her for openers, seeing as how she's government, and so are we. Sort of."

"A lady doctor?" Maddox snapped, his lifelong male

chauvinism baring its fangs. "Goddamn women's lib'll be the death of this country yet. In my day—but let's not get started on that. Speed is essential, so I suppose we're stuck with her. *If* she'll come see Roy, that is."

"One more consideration on the plus side, Maddox. According to my watch, it's two-thirty in the afternoon of Wednesday, April 26."

"Yeah, so?"

"Five gets you ten you won't have to hunt Dr. Messick down on a golf course."

In the days that followed, Roy Ramsdell ascertained the hard way that no matter how many components the human body consisted of, disease managed to develop a specific torment for each. After his first glimpse of Laura Messick, Ramsdell was also interested to learn that one peculiar symptom had superceded all the others:

An unnatural palpitation of the heart began as soon as she entered the room.

If this were illness, he hoped he never recovered. He admitted he should be up and about, getting on with the all-important task the President had placed in his hands. Then he dwelt on Laura and her daily visits, and told himself the project would proceed just as well under Lippert's temporary direction. Maddox could be counted on to work independently, as always. That minimized his contact with the remainder of the group; a few remained wary of the man, Ramsdell knew, aware of his background, his former abrasive clashes with colleagues, the assault, the prison term.

On this particular occasion, Laura was wearing a pink ribbon in her red-gold hair. Ramsdell was able to fill his eyes with her as she read the thermometer she had extracted from Ramsdell's mouth. She flashed a satisfied smile.

"Ninety-nine even, Roy. Almost normal. I'm pleased, I really am, at your progress. Flu bugs can be nasty little animals. Sometimes they hang on forever."

So she's pleased, Ramsdell thought. Well, that goes double for me. Only the kind of progress she's talking about and the kind I have on my mind are two different things. Does she realize she called me by my first name just then? Or was that a slip of the tongue? It's always been "Mr. Ramsdell" and "Dr. Messick," the strictly formal physician-patient relationship.

Ramsdell regarded Laura as cool, professional, efficient, yet every inch a woman, a female of the species such as he'd never encountered before. Not that Ramsdell—intellectual, ivory tower inhabitant, academician, researcher—had led a celibate life. Far from it. His memory dredged up interludes, most of brief duration. He enjoyed sex, the mental and physical release it brought about. It was the time he begrudged, for in Roy Ramsdell's order of priorities, sex ranked far below science and serenity.

In Laura's Messick's case, though, Ramsdell was prepared to make an exception. For the first time in his life, he had fallen deeply and intensely in love. Early on, he elicited the information she was single, unattached, as involved in her medical career as he with his scientific investigation and problem-solving. Ramsdell wondered if Laura reciprocated his devotion even slightly, or if indeed she felt anything for him at all.

"You should be up and about in a couple of days, Roy," said Laura, dropping her stethoscope into the medical kit she carried. "Continue drinking plenty of water and fruit juice; I want your fluid intake to remain high for the present. You can discontinue the medication I prescribed, however. Let nature take over the rest of the curative process now."

"You're the doctor," Ramsdell observed. "And a good one, I might add. How are things going over at Camp Connolly?"

She frowned. "Not as well as I'd expected. We should be further along by now. There are almost a thousand refugees living there already and it's nowhere near finished. More arrive every day, and it's the same all over. Too little too late, then hurry up so everybody can wait. Shortages, snafus, delays. Washington as usual is asking for miracles, but it isn't going to get them. Damn and blast Congress to hell anyway, caving in to public opinion as they did! Let me tell you, this will be one God-awful mess before it's finished."

"You sound like you have a temper to accompany that red hair," Ramsdell said.

"You bet I do. Especially when I see incompetence, fuzzy thinking, above all political expediency in an emergency. It's downright revolting."

"My sentiments exactly. Incidentally, when will you be back? I'm still far from recovered, you know."

"With Camp Connolly in the condition it's in, certainly not tomorrow, and probably not the day after, either. I've got sanitation, food distribution, and construction of the camp dispensary and hospital to worry about, for openers. And you're a charming liar, Roy. You're as healthy as a horse, and I've just removed you from the critical list."

"Guilty," he admitted. "But is it so surprising that a man recently returned from the brink of death wants to check up on his physician's availability?"

"I guess not. Only her availability is going to be severely limited from now on."

"Even to her star patient?"

"I didn't say that, Roy. You're in the middle of a life-and-death struggle against the bees. My battle is with disease and epidemic. Both are vitally important. There won't be enough hours in each day as it is."

"In other words," Ramsdell said, taking the plunge, "unless I succumb to some exotic microbe again, the start of a beautiful friendship is also the end."

Laura reddened. "I didn't say that, either," she murmured. "We both have telephones. You *could* call me once in a while."

They shook hands formally. Laura Messick departed, leaving behind a lingering aura of cologne and scented soap. Leaning back on the pillow, Ramsdell assured himself that Laura had allowed her hand to remain in his longer than cordiality dictated.

It was, he decided, a very good sign.

With Ramsdell out of action and Lippert in charge, Henry Maddox wrestled up to eighteen hours a day with a dwindling list of proposals put forth to check the killer bees from ravishing the North American continent. He tested, analyzed, programmed, read printouts until his eyes rebelled, discarded, started anew.

While Maddox had somewhat softened his previous cantankerous stance against the scientific community, his own branch included, subordinating his prejudices and bigotry in the interests of the common cause, he gained great personal satisfaction from the forces of (to him) poetic justice at work.

The Establishment, which had rejected, pilloried and finally imprisoned him, had in its extremity turned to Henry Maddox to help save it. Daily, he savored the irony of the whole thing more and more.

April 30, 1977

By the millions, they poured across a thousand miles of border between Mexico and the United States, a rushing torrent of humanity with but a single goal in mind: self-preservation. The bees? Still far away. Past failures to halt them? *Los Yanquis* were smart; eventually a light would glow at the end of a dark tunnel. The future? No one knew, nor cared, what tomorrow might bring. For the present, sanctuary to the north of the Rio Grande was all that counted. Was not *Tío Samuel* rich, with many resources? He would provide. *Braceros*, Mexican wetback laborers, were especially pleased; many were entering the United States legally, by invitation, for the first time.

Lost in the tidal wave of displaced persons that inundated Camp Connolly, unnoticed and unknown to each other amid the teeming, chattering mob, were an orphaned white boy and a black Viet Nam veteran.

Each had arrived in Texas by separate routes and for different reasons.

Timmy Benjamin had abandoned his beloved ham radio rig, along with a host of painful memories at the gravesite of his parents, and fled. He had no relatives he could turn to. Costa Rica was a deserted, burnt-out wasteland. America offered—what? Bread and soup and a cot in a DP camp. Timmy admitted it didn't seem like a heck of a lot, but at thirteen, the youthful spirit of adventure bubbled to the top. Besides, what alternative was there? Resolutely, he turned his face northward and, as the saying goes, started putting one foot in front of the other.

To Alonzo Cole, life had lately changed into a series of eccentric jumps from frying pan to fire and back again. The futility of it all appalled him. The panic and upheaval caused by the onrushing bees had made an insane asylum of the whole world, it appeared to Cole. That being the case, one place was pretty much the same as another. Flipping a mental coin, he headed toward the Texas border. Food and shelter were easy to come by. In addition, Cole realized he had one valuable plus in his favor, no matter where he landed. He need worry no longer about supporting a hundred-dollar-a-day heroin habit.

Hard on the heels of the refugees came, not unnaturally, the human vultures who preyed on misery and sought profit from the misfortunes of fellow men, the true camp-followers of the Apocalypse: gamblers, whores, hustlers, con artists, wanted criminals, black market operators, shady dealers in everything from abortions to zodiac readings. All viewed the jerry-built DP cities, and the bee-panicked fugitives they contained, as fertile fields for personal enrichment.

For those coveting the solace of religion, legitimate clergymen and charlatans alike came forward. Night and day, in a dozen places at every refugee camp, services of every conceivable sort were conducted, each Messenger of the Lord surrounded by his own small congregation of faithful. Catholic priests, who enjoyed by far the largest number of communicants. Protestant ministers. Jewish rabbis. Mormon elders. Fundamentalists, literal interpreters of the Bible, who equated the threat of the killer bees with the end of the world, the Day of judgement, a scourge sent by God to cleanse the earth as the flood had.

These latter hurled hellfire-and-damnation sermons at their listeners, advising them their span on earth was short, urging them to prepare for the next life before it was too late.

Despite diversity of approach, all shared a common belief—the sincere conviction they were providing genuine spiritual comfort.

The charlatans, the self-ordained, so-called "men of the cloth" whose titles stemmed from mailorder diploma mills, the greedy who had established "churches" to take advantage of tax loopholes, operated on a far different level. "To support their ministry," as they expressed it, they sold their particular brand of salvation for whatever the traffic would bear. Of buyers, there was no dearth.

Numbered among the "quick buck" religious fraternity was Gerard Montague. Notwithstanding his earlier exit, "The Prophet" could have kissed the soil of the United States when he found himself once again treading on it. His Mexican sojourn he assayed as an unqualified disaster. The natives were Roman Catholic to a man. American tourists didn't stay in one place long enough to fall victim to any of his bunco schemes. He considered Mexican food, on the whole, atrocious; what little he'd eaten had produced a classic case of "Montezuma's Revenge". On the plus side, Montague had been able to persuade a plump, nubile Mexican bird to exchange the poverty of her Chihuahua village for the good life on the U.S. side of the border.

All in all, he reflected, things were working out well. In the natural confusion of setting up the initial refugee camps—the sheer numbers involved, the basic problems of housing, feeding, and health—neither state nor federal officials had the manpower to conduct a search for him. Camp Crockett, on the outskirts of San Angelo, would at its capacity, hold 50,000 people. Already, he'd selected several likely marks for his "money is tainted" pitch; he expected to start cashing in any day. Though jealous, possessive and hot-tempered, Lupe screwed like three minks dipped in Spanish Fly. At last, it seemed to him, he might be in the way of getting it all together.

Leaning against the side of the Volkswagen one night, "The Prophet" stared long and hard at the purpling Texas sky.

"Heavy, man, real heavy, those goddamn bees," he said. "Let the sons of bitches come. By the time they do, I'll be long gone from here. With a pot full of money."

May 1–June 11, 1977

Within the space of forty-two days, their ranks being constantly augmented by the high reproductivity potential of *adansonii* "superbee" mutants, the gigantic pack of multicolored interlopers roared through Nicaragua, El Salvador, Honduras, and British Honduras. By the second week in June, just about on schedule, they reached the frontier between Guatamala and Mexico.

Far below the surface of the earth, in the Nike missile site command post that had become the hub of their existence, Roy Ramsdell and Henry Maddox shared bitter doubts and an equally bitter pot of coffee.

Maddox looked up. "You thinking what I am, Roy?"

"Uh-huh. Especially if you're thinking that the two of us alleged scientific experts don't have enough brains between us to do a long-division arithmetic problem! Experts? Bullshit. We're dummies, that's what we are. Stupid clods. Pseudo-intellectuals kidding ourselves that we're real hotshots."

"That's putting it a little too strong," said Maddox. "You know, you remind me of the character who kept hitting himself over the head with a hammer because it felt so good when he stopped. Well, if the name-calling and breast-beating turn you on, be my guest, let off some steam. But I'll tell you one thing, Roy. I'm sixty years old. It's taken me most of my life to realize how much time I wasted bitching about matters I had no control over."

"I guess you've got a point there, Henry," Ramsdell said. "But it galls the hell out of me that we've been licked by those lousy bees up to here. It's become like a chess game, a very deadly one, not just Fisher and Spassky for the world title. Move. Countermove. Move. Countermove. And I'm afraid it can end only one way. Checkmate. Theirs. Over us."

Maddox drained the last of his coffee. It was amazing how much his appearance had changed. Instead of the flab, Maddox now had a taut, stringy body. His face, now that the booze was gone, looked ten years younger. He snarled, "Abominable stuff. Tastes like the drippings off a grease rack. Wherever you found that alleged head cook of ours, send him back. Seriously, though, I know how you feel. I've been beaten a few times in my life, and I hate it."

"The great American ethic," Ramsdell said. "Win at any cost. Remember what Vince Lombardi said once? 'There's no such thing as second place.' But he was only a football coach. All he had to worry about was the Green Bay Packers. We're involved in a far more serious struggle. Second place for us isn't pleasant to contemplate, since the future of the country's at stake." He rose from the table, commenced pacing furiously.

"Roy, with all the pressure you've had to contend with lately—from the President, the press, God knows who else—it's no wonder you're down, way down. Let me assure you, you've done all that was humanly possible, and then some."

"Fat lot of good it did," Ramsdell said in a savage tone. "First the fiasco at the Canal Zone. Now more of the same the last month and a half. We've consulted with people from Mexico, Guatamala, Honduras. Had the benefit of their thinking. Agreed on a dozen different varieties of control techniques against the bee swarms. And what's been the net result? Zero, Henry. Absolute zero. We're right back where we started, which is nowhere."

"Not precisely true," said Maddox. "At least we've learned what *doesn't* work. Costa Rica's 'scorched earth,' for instance. Chemical sprays such as the arsenical group, plus almost all the others usually considered effective on bees, from aldrin to zinophos. Army chemical warfare gases containing nervous system and sensory perception disorientation components. Aerial drops of microencapsulated toxicants. Dissemination of AFB. Bombing runs with liquid napalm. You're right, Roy. All have failed, or at the very most been moderately successful. Now, carry the analysis one step further. What is the single common denominator? Why have we come up empty so many times?"

Ramsdell stopped pacing, stood in front of Maddox. "Of course!" he said, smiting himself on the forehead. "'Moderately successful' is the key phrase. Control measures that should stop bees in a few commercial hives or an apiary will never do us any good, *simply because of the numbers we're dealing with*. We kill one Africanized hybrid, and before we know it, ten more are being born to take their places tenfold! The heat, the bees' reproductive frenzy, maybe some other factors we don't know anything about yet."

"Exactly," Maddox said. "Go to the head of the class. Since the Canal Zone, chances are the bee mass has doubled in size. How many did that Mexican entomologist, Urruca, estimate? Ten billion, twenty billion? Even using the most lethal substances known to man, how can we put any kind of substantial, permanent dent in a herd that size?"

"So what's the answer then, Henry?"

"I don't have one. Except to fall back on that motheaten cliché about doing the difficult immediately, and taking a little longer with the impossible. Or perhaps express the forlorn hope that the ecological-environmental imbalance we'be been battling will right itself by some unexpected natural process. Christ knows, everything we've had to contend with has been *un*natural enough! The heat, the bees, the necessity for improvising defenses against an invading force never encountered before." Maddox laughed bitterly, a harsh sound that contained no hint of mirth. "The law of averages has *got* to start operating again one day. A balancing of the scales, so to speak. And may that day arrive soon! Goddamn it, Roy, we've been kicked around long enough."

Ramsdell sat down again. He and Maddox stared at each other silently. Their thoughts were far from pleasant, their prospects bleak, their responsibilities awesome in the face of a fast-approaching deadline.

Five months, or less.

The bees had hit Mexico on the 11th of June, confirming the amazingly accurate projection Secretary of Agriculture Jarvis had given to the President back in February.

Unless something interrupted their flight, they would be at the Rio Grande River in 150 days.

June 14, 1977

EXCERPT FROM THE ABC-TV EVENING NEWS, VIEWED THROUGHOUT THE COUNTRY ON THE AFFILIATE STATIONS OF THE AMERICAN BROADCASTING COMPANY NETWORK.

REASONER: "And now with tonight's commentary, here's Howard K. Smith.

SMITH: "In three weeks, in the normal course of events, the United States would have observed the two-hundred and first anniversary of its independence from England. However, the course of events the American people are currently undergoing cannot in any sense of the word be considered normal. The nation finds itself more enslaved and enchained by the incredible phenomenon of the bees than it ever was in even the darkest hours of King George's tyranny.

"The Latin writer Marcus Tullius Cicero bemoaned 'the times and the standards.' Were he alive today, he undoubtedly would have repeated the same phrase, with equal justification. Thomas Paine spoke of 'the times that try mens' souls.'

"Make no mistake about it, the American people are being sorely tried, and the accompanying relaxation of the country's moral fibre is alarming to behold. A spirit of 'eat, drink, be merry, for tomorrow we die' is upon the land.

"Although we lack a week until the official calendar advent of summer, average daily temperatures of 100°, from Alaska to Maine, from San Diego to Miami, have provided the most blistering spring on record.

"The population is swollen by an estimated twenty-five million refugees in makeshift camps, or 'DP cities' if you will, scattered throughout every thinly populated state west of the Mississippi. More arrive daily, posing vast and nearly insurmountable problems for the federal government, which solemnly assured them they would be welcome here.

"Inflation has risen to the double-digit levels of 1973 and 1974, with no letup in sight. Our neighboring lands to the south are devastated, empty, burnt-out ruins. This has caused many staples to all but disappear from the American table—meats, coffee, bananas, sugar. In a domino effect, food prices continue to skyrocket as shortages, profiteering and black market activities take their toll.

"Finally, and perhaps most alarming of all, there seems to be a breakdown in morality, accelerating in direct proportion to the coming of the day of reckoning. Not to belabor the obvious, the vast columns of bees are in Mexico at this very minute, driving steadily northeastward. Hand in hand with the gradual obliteration of ethical, moral, and legal yardsticks has come a growing reluctance on the part of the populace to rely on duly constituted authorities to administer justice, maintain law and order. Almost hourly fresh reports are received of vigilante committees, barrelhead courts, hangings and other types of summary executions.

"For those of us who love the United States, who remember her as the splendid place she once was (and I think it's safe to say we constitute an overwhelming majority), these events make a sickening mockery of those ideals that are the foundation of our republic.

"It is indeed fortunate none of the founding fathers are able to return and walk the earth again. To a man, they would be ashamed of their handiwork.

"Harry."

June 16, 1977

Roy Ramsdell, Henry Maddox, and the rest of the Irregulars were nothing if not realistic.

After a night-long discussion in the command post, they reached a commonsense decision. They started with the premise that up to now, no new formula for containing, delaying, halting, or wiping out the bees had been devised. Since that condition existed, and might well continue, the possibility then became very strong that the bees would enter the United States. If they did, the next logical step lay in protecting the population from the potentially deadly effects of being stung by *adansonii*. That, it was decided, meant mass innoculations with anti-bee venom serum. In the endeavor, Henry Maddox took the lead.

Spearheading a crash program begun some weeks before, Maddox had at last found what he was searching for, the "ace in the hole" as he and Ramsdell called it.

Maddox conducted test after complicated test on laboratory animals, and, at length, human volunteers. Their results convinced Maddox that a viable serum could be obtained from centrifuged and cultured blood specimens of those who had suffered stings and survived. Innoculation with but a small quantity of the resultant serum, thousands of experiments proved, served to protect most people, even those unfortunates known to possess hypersensitivity, the so-called "anaphylactic reaction," to bee stings.

The President turned out to be an unexpected stumbling block.

"Is it really necessary, Roy?" he demanded on the telephone, as Ramsdell sought approval from the Chief Executive to start setting up the immunization program.

"We must face facts, Mr. President. If the bees get through, failure to carry out mass innoculations would be signing the death warrants of hundreds and thousands of citizens. Personally, I don't want that on my conscience. I don't believe you do either."

"Naturally not." The Preisdent paused a moment. "It's just . . . well, to put it frankly, that speech of mine. Asking our people to take injections of anti-bee venom is like admitting defeat, giving up, telling them they've been lied to and let down. The implications could be very serious in terms of hysteria, mass panic, and so forth."

"I understand, sir," said Ramsdell. "But they'll have to be told the truth sooner or later. And the truth is, right now my group is fighting a losing war. Give Americans the straight dope, they'll usually listen."

"Exactly the point, Roy. I don't think the time is ripe for us to disclose how precarious our position is." He coughed discreetly.

Ramsdell's patience snapped. Was he hearing right? With the lives of countless numbers of innocent bystanders at stake, could it be possible this normally tough-minded, outspoken man was vacillating? Keeping an ear attuned to shifting political winds in such a dreadful time of crisis?

"Mr. President," Ramsdell said, a hint of coldness in his voice, "I am a scientific researcher and you're an elected public official. We each do our job as we see it. I don't know one damn thing about politics, nor do I want to, because even at best, it's a filthy business. You entrusted me with a specific task some months ago, and I'm carrying it out to the best of my ability. Until or unless you see fit to replace me, I'll continue to do just that. Therefore, Mr. President, I urge you most strongly to give me the green light on the innoculation program."

A lengthy pause ensued on the Washington end of the line. Then the President said, "Oh, very well, Roy, go ahead with it. I'll give you all the help I can spare from the Public Health Service. But treat the whole program as simply a precautionary measure."

"Yes, Mr. President. Thank you, sir. And good night."

June 19, 1977

By radio, TV, newspapers, billboards, posters, all the various media for mass communication, in English, Spanish, and several other languages throughout the refugee camps and the country at large, the call went out for bee sting survivors to report to designated medical authorities for blood sampling.

At Camp Connolly, long ragged lines of those responding to the appeal stretched as far as the eye could see. Lines began at the barbed-wire fencing around the enclosure's perimeter and snaked all the way to the central mess hall, a distance of over half a mile.

His dark skin glistening with sweat in the intense heat of summertime Texas, Alonzo Cole wondered what in the world he was doing there, standing in an endless, shuffling procession, waiting to have a needle stuck in his arm, just because "whitey" had asked him to. Briefly, he remembered the wretched years (as he now realized they had been) when needles comprised an integral part of his existence, instruments of escape from reality. In the old days, Cole never would have thought it possible to function without heroin. "Once a junkie, always a junkie" was the axiom of the streets. Sure, a man might kick for a while, but sooner or later he'd be back on the stuff.

"This is one dude they ain't jivin' with all that garbage," Cole muttered softly, inching forward another foot or so. "I kicked, even if I didn't know I was doin' it. And

I'm gonna stay clean this time. How long's it been now? Almost three months. Jesus, ain't that something!"

Cole became aware of being under scrutiny from the person immediately ahead of him in the line, a sturdily built, sad-faced boy of perhaps thirteen or fourteen.

"Were you talking to me, mister?" he inquired.

Cole shook his head. "Uh-uh. Jus' kind of rambling on to myself, you might say. Why? You want to rap, kid? Help to pass the time. It's going to be a hell of a wait until we get into that mess hall. You musta been stung by bees or you wouldn't be here. Where'd it happen to you?"

Without warning, the youngster shuddered, and Cole was amazed to note tears welling up in his brown eyes. He fought to suppress them, finally gave up the struggle and yielded openly to his emotions.

Cole placed a hand on the boy's shoulder. "Go ahead, kid, let it all out," he said. "I done some of that not so very long ago myself. I found out I ain't any less a man for it. Name's Alonzo Cole, case you're interested."

"Timmy's mine. Timmy Benjamin."

For the next two hours, as they stood together in the broiling sun, the orphaned lad from a Costa Rican coffee plantation and the war-hardened ex-addict who had once called Harlem home engaged each other in conversation, exchanged experiences and found themselves cementing a strange and unlikely friendship.

Despite the wide difference in their backgrounds, education, speech patterns, thought processes, life styles, Alonzo Cole and Timmy Benjamin came to conclude they shared a common bond. Besides the bees and the manner in which they had affected each, there was the knowledge they coexisted in a world of misery and danger.

Neither could predict when even that tenuous condition might abruptly end; their only certainty was uncertainty.

June 20-July 10, 1977

Major chemical combines, manufacturers of pharmaceuticals, ethical drug companies, and private and commercial laboratories all bent to the monumental task of providing sufficient anti-bee venom serum to innoculate an entire population, plus several million invited guests. Despite the impossibility of the logistics, the great conglomeration of humanity involved, and the inevitable foul-ups, a surprisingly large percentage of Americans received their shots. Lavish in its praise, the press called the effort "the most widespread mass immunization program ever undertaken in medical history." Compliance was voluntary; most accepted the necessity without demur. Others did not, through apathy, fear, or religious convictions.

Fundamentalists and their converts, plus a few other splinter sects, seized the opportunity to extend their influence on a nationwide basis. They picketed innoculation stations night and day, ringing them with chanting, shouting groups of wild-eyed zealots. They quoted scripture to prove such invasions of the body against the will of God, Who, they reiterated, wanted the earth cleansed of wicked mankind for once and for all.

In such scattered urban centers as Detroit, New Orleans, Phoenix, and Boston, large-scale riots ensued, scores of arrests were made, with injuries and deaths reported. Impressed by the seemingly sincere advocates of noncompliance, some changed their minds, refused immunization. The remainder submitted fatalistically.

Notwithstanding the "only a precautionary measure" tag appended to the innoculation program by both the President and Roy Ramsdell, most viewed the maneuver (as the President had feared) as a tacit admission on the part of the government that the gigantic bee swarm could probably not be dealt with as promised.

FROM THE EDITORIAL PAGE OF THE SALT LAKE
CITY *DESERET EVENING NEWS:*

"We applaud the forthrightness and courage with
which the White House approached the recent mass
innoculations of anti-bee venom serum. We congrat-
ulate the United States Public Health Service, the
American Medical Association, and individual members of the medical fraternity for the dispatch with
which they executed the immense task.

"Nevertheless, in its wake we must note several
disheartening aftereffects, not only here on the shores
of the Great Salt Lake but in the other forty-nine
states as well.

"Public confidence in elected officials, particularly
those in Washington, has sunk to a low level unparal-
leled since the dreary days of the Nixon-Watergate
mess. Rightly or wrongly, public opinion holds the
President personally responsible for failure to devise
adequate countermeasures against the imminent invasion of the killer bees, now reported moving in a solid
wall five to ten miles long somewhere in Mexico.

"The *Deseret Evening News* cannot concur in this
belief. We feel the well-known scientific investigator-
researcher Roy Ramsdell, appointed by the President
some months ago to head up a halt-the-bees team, has
done as well as could be expected in unprecedented
circumstances. On how many occasions in the past
have man's best efforts, even the most brilliant and
well-conceived, proven puny indeed when opposed to
the forces of nature gone mad?

"Additional unpleasant manifestations of apathy and
a desire to pass whatever months, weeks, days, or
hours remain in hedonistic debauchery grip much of
the nation. How one chooses to while away what he
considers the last of his life had become contingent
upon financial condition, it seems.

"The rich in the big cities drink hundred-dollar
bottles of champagne and hold sex orgies with thou-
sand-dollar call girls, inflation being what it is today.

The poor listen to their favorite 'End of the World' or 'Day of Judgment' preachers, and await their premature ascent to the Pearly Gates with what equanimity they can muster. Never has the gap yawned wider between 'haves' and 'havenots.' Such polarization of society isn't healthy at any time. Its current implications are even less so."

The editorial sentiment of the *Deseret Evening News* was echoed in a dozen other newspapers across the land as July drew toward its close.

July 11, 1977

Driving across the miles separating the Nike missile site from Camp Connolly, Roy Ramsdell was struck with the singular beauty of the stars, the sky, the jutting Santiago Mountains, even the parched plain that rolled northward to the horizon. Despite his own growing sense of frustration and impatience at the failure of the Irregulars to come up with a successful formula against the bees, Ramsdell had gained a sense of peace from his meditative discipline. Did he not, he asked himself, merit a few stolen moments of R&R, the same as everyone else, amid the crumbling fragments of their world? Could it be termed a run-of-the-mill occurrence when a man in love for the first time suddenly found that love returned? He decided it couldn't, and conjured up a vision of Laura Messick.

When they were face to face, the image shifted to an entirely different one. Obviously, a medical emergency of major proportions was in progress.

Coughing, wheezing, sweating patients filled every bed in the tiny hospital, lay on stretchers in aisles and corridors, stood huddled outside in blanket-covered misery. Overworked, spread too thin because there simply weren't enough of them, tottering with fatigue, Laura and her staff resembled haggard, gray-faced zombies. Doctors, nurses, orderlies, paramedical volunteers, and technicians tried in vain to cope with a flood of sufferers that threatened to engulf them all.

Ramsdell finally gained Laura's attention, motioning toward the doorway of her makeshift office. He noticed she almost fell crossing the room; she appeared to be walking in her sleep. Up close, her appearance was even more appalling to Ramsdell: eyes red-rimmed, features puffy, hair untidy. Still and all, he thought, she had to be the most beautiful woman he'd ever seen. Laura shut the door behind her, and without preamble rushed into his enfolding arms, sobbing dejectedly against his shoulder.

Aghast, Ramsdell said, "My God, Laura! What have you got out there, an epidemic? Is the whole place coming down with the same malady simultaneously?"

"It looks like it, Roy darling. New cases every hour. I've had phone calls from the doctors at Camps Houston, Crockett, Travis, and San Jacinto. They report hundreds of refugees with similar complaints. Epidemic? I guess so. You couldn't have used a more apt word."

"Of what disease?"

"We aren't sure yet. With all these people living in such close contact, it'll be difficult to check the spread, no matter how fast we isolate the specific organism causing it. It could be one of a dozen things. All we know at the moment is, it's characterized by marked URI symptoms. . . ."

"URI?" Ramsdell said with a puzzled expression.

"Medicalese for 'Upper Respiratory Infection.' Personally, I lean toward pneumococcic pneumonia. With no lab here, I had to send sputum specimens into Alpine and Sanderson for analysis. Until the correct diagnosis is established, we won't be able to institute the proper treatment. In the first place, penicillin is in dreadfully short supply everywhere. More important, many strains of pneumonia bacilli have grown totally impervious to penicillin therapy. Using it to combat them'd be about as effective as plain water or a normal saline solution."

Ramsdell nodded. "You do have a problem, all right."

"Make that plural. This is simply the latest of many."

The telephone rang, its jangle startlingly loud within the confines of the small office. Laura Messick snatched it up, listened briefly, murmured, "Thanks, I appreciate it," turned back to Ramsdell.

"That was the lab in Alpine. The one in Sanderson arrived at the same result independently, they told me. Pneumococcic pneumonia. Cultures and stained slides confirmed it. In other circumstances, we'd be able to proceed full speed ahead to bring this outbreak under control." Laura paused, gnawing at her lower lip.

"Then in this case, the shortage of penicillin is critical?" Ramsdell asked.

"You bet it is, Roy. We don't have enough on hand to treat half our pneumonia patients."

Later, after Ramsdell had left (how brief the moments they shared, she thought, and how much she'd come to love him!), Laura called Dr. Klein in Washington. She realized it might be a useless gesture, but one she had to make in the interests of humanity, let alone her obligations as a doctor.

He sounded irritable and fully as tired as she. "Laura I'm aware you need penicillin desperately. As well as the fact we don't have any to give you. To put it bluntly, we're tapped out. The Surgeon General's scouring every source, domestic and foreign, for additional supplies. When we do find any, the price is outrageous. We pay it anyway, even though it sticks in our craws, these unconscionable hijackers holding us up, taking advantage of the bind we're in."

"Then the answer is no, Dr. Klein?" Laura yelled. "What the hell am I supposed to do here? Pat my patients on the head, and ease them as gently as possible into The Great Beyond untreated? Is that what you're suggesting? Because if it is, I'm ready to resign from the medical profession *and* the human race at the same time. I'm afraid the glib, detached bedside manner they prattled about in medical school wouldn't be up to it."

"Laura, you always choose the worst times to tilt at

windmills!" She knew her superior was struggling for self-control. "But, suppose for the sake of argument I could lay my hands on five hundred cases. Would that help?"

For a few seconds, his words didn't register. "You mean of penicillin?"

"What did you think? Orange marmalade? Of course, penicillin. Ampules. In aqueous solution."

"No, Dr. Klein," Laura said, excited now. "It wouldn't help. Much. Just save countless lives, that's all, ours included. To say nothing of containing the brushfire possibilities of an epidemic like this. Where is it, and how soon can you get it here?"

"If the Surgeon General ever finds out about it, I might as well hop the first outbound jet. I'm robbing Peter to pay Paul, as it is. The five hundred cases are in a warehouse in Dallas. Some outfit called International Trading Corporation. INTCO, for short. Owned by some guy named Hagman, Hogson, Hegerman, something like that."

July 15, 1977

Like a triumphant, all-conquering army, troops of an Alexander or Napoleon subjugating the peoples they encountered, the bees were completing the process of overrunning Mexico. The government had at last fled across the Rio Grande, counseling its few remaining citizens to do the same, and abandoning the country to the invaders. Thus, with no human or natural agency to impede their progress, the bees swarmed up through Chiapas and Oaxaca, past the Isthmus of Tehuantepec, to occupy the lower portion of the Federal District and the capital.

Obtaining the cooperation of the Mexican government-in-exile through the United States Department of State, Roy Ramsdell had had placed at his disposal a Mexican

Air Force helicopter. Since Ramsdell wished to make a firsthand reconnaissance of the bee migration as it then stood, he prevailed upon Kent Grayson to fly him to Mexico City. An aeronautical engineer by profession and a pilot by avocation, Grayson was the Irregulars' expert on everything that flew, from World War II P-38's to 747's.

The two observers swooped in low from the northeast, following the toll road from Ectapec, past El Tepeyac Park, hovered momentarily above the point where Insurgentes Norte and Calzada de los Misterios intersected.

"See any signs of them yet, Roy?" Grayson shouted tensely, above the thunderous throb of the chopper's power plant.

"Negative. Anyway, our latest intelligence says they're farther south. And west." He jabbed a thumb in that direction. "Swing over toward Chapultepec Park."

Long before they reached the beautiful verdant acreage, named by the Aztecs for its resemblance to a grasshopper sitting on a hill, they caught sight of the enemy. Instead of half the city, he had infested nearly two-thirds, advance units having already fanned out to alight in Alameda Park and the Hacienda Athletic Club. The Arena de Mexico also was submerged under a dark, undulating mass.

The *ahuehuete* trees in Chapultepec Park, some 200-feet tall, groaned under the weight of millions of bees. They clung to the gossamer Spanish moss like clusters of grapes. Most of the animals of the zoo were dead, deserted by the flight of their keepers, victims of hunger, thirst, bee stings. A short distance away, the Botanical Gardens held millions more of the tawny-furred insects. The city flower market at the Calzada Tacubaya entrance to the park had also claimed its share of attention from hordes of hungry *adansonii* specimens.

From Chapultepec Park, Ramsdell and the nervous Grayson fluttered south, through Coyoacan and Villa Obregón, then cut east to Tepepan and Xochimilco. In whichever direction they traveled, it was the same story. Every square inch of Mexico City that contained grass and flowers (which meant most of the capital, actually) was bee-infested. Nothing could be seen of the famed Floating Gardens at Xochimilco except a constantly shifting carpet of bees, feasting on the fragrant blossoms. Occasionally, their labors disturbed by the helicopter's rotor noises, a dense cloud of bees rose into the air, like an errant puff of dust from a rural road, investigated briefly, then settled back down again.

To Roy Ramsdell, the strategy of the swarm was obvious. They appeared to be in another of their feeding frenzies, stoking up their honey stomachs on the lush flora of the Mexican Peninsula in anticipation of their next forward leap. They had followed a similar pattern before; by now, it was a familiar routine. Perhaps they sensed that vegetation in their path would be scarce, perhaps not. At any rate, they were moving at a slightly accelerated pace. They might reach the Rio Grande prior to the mid-November estimate. The thought chilled an already dispirited Roy Ramsdell.

He signaled Grayson, pointing north. "I've seen enough, Kent. Let's get the hell out of here. Take her back to the barn."

On the return trip Grayson was silent, relieved to be going away from danger. Ramsdell folded his arms and hid his apprehensions behind his sunglasses. He fretted over his own lack of progress. Worried about Laura. Wondered what Maddox's reaction to his news from the Mexican capital would be.

Nagging, insignificant anxieties, Ramsdell assured himself, when measured against the big picture. None would really matter, in the long run. Not unless they came up with something, *anything* useful, and quickly. If they didn't, life as they had known it could grind to a halt within the next eighty days.

July 20, 1977

"I don't understand it, Roy," Laura Messick said sadly. "I don't understand it at all." They stood outside the dispensary at Camp Connolly. She looked more harassed, more frightened now than previously. She was wringing her slender hands; the knuckles were white under her tanned skin. Even her usually glowing hair looked dull.

"You mean the penicillin not proving effective?"

"Yes. Frankly, I'm baffled. Not only have we failed to clear up the old cases, new ones keep cropping up. It's completely out of hand. As I mentioned before, some pneumonia bacilli thrive and multiply on penicillin, because they've developed a genetic immunity. But unless it's happened just lately, pneumococcic organisms have never been in that category. Good God, Roy, what am I going to do? I can't treat, cure, or even isolate for lack of space. Can I order my patients to stop breathing on each other? That'll occur soon enough in any event."

"How's the boy doing?" Ramsdell asked. "You know, the one you told me had become a favorite of everybody on your staff."

"You mean Timmy Benjamin?" She shook her head. "Poor, I'm afraid. Does a thirteen-year-old kid whose parents were killed by the bees in Costa Rica need pneumonia too? No, of course not. But he has it. And we can't stabilize him. Temp remains elevated, rales in both lungs, consolidation, all the classic symptoms. Massive doses of penicillin, to the point both arms and his seat resemble pincushions. And still nothing. I'd have to classify Timmy as critical, and not improving at all."

A suspicion began to form in Ramsdell's mind, based on hunch and intuition rather than scientific deduction or hard facts. Besides, he'd read of similar situations before, in Korea, Viet Nam, post-World War II Germany. They hadn't just happened accidentally. Someone had *made* them happen.

112

"Laura, dearest," he said, "What I'm about to suggest will shock you, but it all seems to lock in. Your penicillin isn't doing the job it's supposed to. Did you ever consider the possibility the drug itself might be defective? Tampered with in some manner? Even deliberately diluted?"

She stared at him for several seconds as the impact of his words sank in, then whispered, "Oh, my God! Roy, you can't be serious! You mean—with all the desperately ill people we—no human being would—no, I can't bring myself to believe it."

"I think you may have to, eventually. These are chaotic times. Lawlessness and disorder all over. Authority has gone down the tube. It's a perfect setup for the greedy. What better way to make a double profit than to cut the strength of a penicillin shipment in half, so you can sell the same amount twice? Where did this stuff come from?"

"Why, a warehouse in Dallas. International Trading something-or-other. Dr. Klein told me on the telephone, but I was so tired that night I can't recall." She struggled to dredge up a fading memory. Suddenly, she wheeled on Ramsdell. "Hey, wait a minute, Roy. At the very end, he ran a string of names by me. What *were* they? 'Harrelson?' No. 'Haggerty?' Uh-uh, not that either. 'Hogson!' Yes, now I remember! 'Hogson!' "

"Who's he?"

"One of the names Dr. Klein mentioned. Owns the company whose warehouse the penicillin was in. If he and a certain Howard Hogson I met in Galveston a few months back during the bubonic plague outbreak are one and the same, I *could* almost credit him with a rotten stunt like this. Roy, he was absolutely the most objectionable individual I've ever run across! Loud-mouthed, profane, bragging of important connections in Washington, the whole works."

"Sounds like a real winner, your Mr. Hogson. Lousy bastard!" Ramsdell considered a moment. "But before we jump to any conclusions without solid evidence, let's take a reading on the penicillin. We have a small lab over at the Nike site. Nothing fancy, but we can handle a simple analysis such as solution strength. Give me a few samples, selected at random from several of the boxes. As soon as we know one way or the other, I'll get back to you."

Three hours later, Ramsdell emerged from his meditation break and went into the lab.

"No doubt about the results, Roy," the lab man said. "Just as you suspected. It's been cut. Fifty percent."

"Thanks, Earl. Disgusting. Really disgusting. Trading lives for money, I mean."

Ramsdell wasted no time in passing the information along to Laura, as he'd promised.

"So that's how it breaks down, Laura," he said, forced to shout over an incredibly bad telephone connection. "Every ampule marked three-hundred-thousand units actually contains only a hundred and fifty. You'll have to double the dosage."

"I can't, Roy. We're running out. I used so much more in the beginning when my patients weren't responding, and they've been on the therapy longer, too."

"Could you try double-dosing only the most serious cases, depend on luck and nature to pull the rest through?"

"I suppose so. I've got to do something. But why must I be forced into the position of playing God, withholding life from some, granting it to others? Damn the Howard Hogsons of this world anyhow!" Sick and tired of the whole sordid affair, emotionally drained, revolted by the treachery, greed, and venality the lab report had laid directly on the doorstep of Hogson's warehouse, Laura Messick disintegrated into incoherent sobs.

Unable to find adequate words of comfort, helpless to do anything except silently empathize with the woman he'd learned to love, Ramsdell held the phone and rode out the storm. At length, Laura's tears subsided, vaporized in a white-hot blast of anger.

"So help me, Roy, doctor or no doctor, if I had a second chance I'd never give that fat slob Hogson a plague antitoxin shot! And if any of my patients die, it'll be Hogson who killed them just as surely as if he'd stabbed or shot them in cold blood! Adulterated pencillin! How low can a person stoop? And Timmy Benjamin. It's still touch and go with him. He may make it, he may not. A thirteen-year-old kid with a whole lifetime ahead of him. Isn't that sickening?"

"Laura, you know you're not supposed to become personally involved with your patients," said Ramsdell. "It's one of the first. . . ."

"I don't give a damn!" Laura exploded. "I do and I am! And when I stop, I'll also cease using M.D. after my name! Let me tell you something, Roy Ramsdell. People like Howard Hogson should be stood up against a wall and shot, no trial—nothing. Not that I presume for one minute it'll ever happen. His kind are usually insulated from justice by their layers of money. Well, I've got to run. Try to salvage what I can from the wreckage."

She abruptly broke the connection, leaving a heartsick Ramsdell to question how much longer he could bear the double burden of his own problems and Laura's grief.

Simultaneously with Ramsdell's call to Laura, Alonzo Cole had entered the hospital to seek out Dr. Messick, inquire about the chances of his newfound acquaintance, Timmy Benjamin.

Several times, he had pondered the validity of his relationship with a white boy; ingrained racial attitudes were tough barriers to overcome. Cole never did sort out the intricate whys and wherefores to his satisfaction. He figured his enforced break with drugs might be part of the answer. Without heroin, a man could get his head together, reason, think more clearly, even discard old prejudices.

Thus it came about that Cole, without intending to eavesdrop, merely standing in the vicinity waiting for Dr. Messick to finish talking on the telephone, overheard her entire conversation with Ramsdell.

July 25, 1977

In a last-ditch attempt to augment their own group efforts against the onrushing bees with a fresh slant and with new input from beyond the tightly knit circle of the irregulars, Ramsdell and Maddox conceived a novel idea.

By phone and by cable, stressing the urgency for attendance the two men called an unprecedented meeting at the underground Texas command post. Invited were all the top entomologists and apiologists of the world, specialists acknowledged as geniuses in their respective countries. Ramsdell and Maddox agreed it represented a desperation move. Nonetheless, both hoped that minds other than theirs, so close to the losing campaign for so long, might possibly turn up a startling concept previously overlooked.

Addressing the seventy or so luminaries assembled in the Nike site at the start of the conference, Henry Maddox spelled out its purpose succinctly.

"As it stands now, gentlemen, the United States is doomed to go the same route as South America, Central America, and Mexico. If the United States succumbs, then Canada will also. Eventually Alaska, next Russia, and finally the rest of Europe will be overrun. Not even the remotest corner of the globe will be spared in years to come. It is up to us to jointly prevent this imminent disaster."

Neither Maddox nor Ramsdell wasted much time on speech-making, for the obvious reason so little time remained. In short order, the initial session broke up into seminars, discussion groups, small clumps of men gathered around charts and blackboards.

Throughout the better part of a night and day, they argued, raised their voices, advanced suggestions, tossed them out as impractical, all in a half-dozen different languages. In the main, the ideas represented merely a rehash of measures already tried and found wanting in Central America. Ramsdell sensed that their longshot wasn't destined to enter the winner's circle.

July 26, 1977

At 4:30 in the morning, nearly twenty-four hours after they had gaveled it to order, Ramsdell and Maddox gave up, declaring the conference at the end. They had made no progress. Instead, the meeting had fragmented into name-calling, futile wrangling, personality clashes, still in a half-dozen different languages. All they had learned was . . . they had learned nothing new.

For the United States of America, less than seventy days of life remained.

July 30, 1977

Standing several days before at the bedside of the critically ill Timmy Benjamin, gazing down at the frail form breathing with labored difficulty even beneath the oxygen tent, Alonzo Cole put into proper perspective Dr. Messick's evaluation of Timmy's condition.

The doctor was right. If Timmy died, it would be murder, pure and simple. Cole conceded he'd been guilty of many acts of which he had no cause to be proud. Fragging gold braid in 'Nam. Taking drugs. Stealing and mugging to purchase heroin. And when he had killed, Cole rationalized, a good and sufficient reason was usually involved: because someone was an enemy, because Cole was being paid to seek out and destroy that enemy, or because an officer's cowardice had cost the lives of buddies needlessly.

But this? Condemning an innocent boy to gasp his life away? Just to clutch a few more tainted dollars?

"No way, man," Cole whispered to himself. "No fuckin' way." He reached under the edge of the oxygen tent, covered a white hand with his own black one. Timmy stirred, but did not open his eyes.

Having reached a decision, Cole moved without delay to implement it.

He checked the Army-issue .45 caliber Colt automatic he wore in a shoulder harness, concealed by his jacket. Stole a fast, late-model car from a gas station lot within walking distance of Camp Connolly. Roared off into the night toward Dallas, 400 miles to the northeast.

Cole considered himself a man with a twin mission, its two objectives vital and inseparable.

Avenge Timmy Benjamin. Snuff Howard Hogson.

August 1-2, 1977

Once again, the nation's journalists and editors had a field day. It is a truism of the trade that good news sells no papers.

INTERNATIONAL CONFERENCE FAILS TO FIND BEE SOLUTION; OUTLOOK GRIM—*Denver Post.*

RAMSDELL TALKS WITH PRESIDENT AT WHITE HOUSE; ADMITS 'IRREGULARS' CANNOT HALT BEES—*Las Vegas Sun.*

STATE OF EMERGENCY EXISTS, SAYS PRESIDENT—*San Antonio Light.*

PRESIDENT ADVISES 'EXTRA PRECAUTIONS' IN ADDITION TO ANTI-BEE VENOM INNOCULATIONS—*Kansas City Star.*

BUILD UNDERGROUND SHELTERS, PRESIDENT BIDS PEOPLE, WE WILL NOT EVACUATE—*Little Rock Traveller.*

PRESIDENT: 'USE MATERIALS AT HAND—BRICKS, ROCKS, WOOD, CEMENT, METAL'—*Chicago Tribune.*

SUBWAYS, GARAGES, BASEMENTS, AIR RAID SHELTERS CAN HOLD MILLIONS, SAY CD OFFICIALS—*Detroit Free Press.*

GOVERNMENT TO STEP UP MANUFACTURE OF BEE PROTECTION SUITS—*Washington Post.*

POLICE, FIREMEN, MUNICIPAL WORKERS WILL HAVE PRIORITY ON PROTECTIVE CLOTHING—*Norfolk Virginian-Pilot.*

'MAIN JOB NOW IS SURVIVAL,' PRESIDENT TELLS NATION—*New London* (Ct.) *Day.*

August 3, 1977

To the one-dimensional mind of Howard Hogson, it was business as usual, bees or no bees.

For nine days, he had flitted in the Lear jet from West Berlin to Paris to Rome to Brussels, buying, selling, haggling, wheeling and dealing, dipping greedy fingers in a dozen deals involving drugs, oil, tanker leases, a consignment of scarce copper. He dined in the best restaurants, drank the most expensive wines, bedded the willing young women provided by his fawning European contacts. Nights, he slept soundly, drifting off not by counting sheep but by calculating the enormous amount of gold Swiss francs deposited to his credit in a numbered Geneva account. If anyone lived the good life, he most certainly did, Hogson assured himself.

Returning to Dallas, Hogson dismissed his chauffeur, inserted a key into the front door of his half-million dollar home, and dropped matched Louis Vuitton luggage on the foyer rug. He wondered where Wilson was; his valet usually greeted him. After all, he *had* been sent a cablegram.

"Wilson!" Hogson thundered. "Wilson! Where the hell are you?"

The echoes of his own voice bounced back to him. Of Wilson there was so sign.

"Funny," Hogson muttered. "I know he takes a nip now and then, but this is ridiculous." His voice rose again. "Wilson!"

A pair of legs slowly began to descend the spiral staircase to the left, feet and ankles appearing first, then calves, knees and thighs.

"It's about time, you old black rascal. Bring me a bourbon on the rocks. Gotta celebrate one hell of a profitable trip." Hogson smiled, projected new deals and more millions to be made now that he was back in "Big D." Suddenly his face froze. He realized the entire scene was wrong—terribly, drastically wrong.

The feet were encased in a muddy pair of paratroop boots, the legs covered by some sort of jungle camouflage material.

"Y'all ain't—y'all ain't . . ." the corpulent Texan stammered.

"As a matter of fact, I'm not," Alonzo Cole said pleasantly, the rest of him coming into view. The automatic, held in a steady hand, pointed directly at Hogson's belt buckle. "I gave Brother Wilson the evening off, when he tipped me you were due in tonight."

"You did what?" Hogson said in astonishment, resuming his customary bluster. The tableau had become clear to him now. Lawless times, desperate men, hunger, narcotics—who knew? Just another routine robbery attempt. Well, if money was what this hard-looking buck was after, he could just take some and be on his way. "Hey, how come y'all know so much about my household staff?"

"Why not? I've had better 'n a week to put it all together, man. *And* promise your chauffeur a piece of the action, so don't count on him to interfere. Besides, he's in the garage, and that's half a mile away."

"Goddamn Nigra," Hogson said under his breath. Then, aloud, "Let's get on with it. There's about fifteen hundred in my wallet. Watch. Diamond ring. Cuff links. If that ain't enough, I got a wall safe upstairs holding ten, twelve thousand." Hogson sneered. "It's only money. Plenty more where that came from."

"Yeah, right on, Hogson, you miserable motherfucker. Maybe another dozen warehouses full of watered penicillin, huh?"

At that instant, Hogson received the first concrete hint that robbery was merely the tip of the iceberg; death, rather than a run-of-the-mill heist, might be in the offing. His eyes darted this way and that, seeking a means of escape. Then he remembered. In the wall safe. His .357 Magnum. If he could. . . .

"What's that about penicillin?" Hogson said, stalling for time. He'd caught the drift immediately. The load in Number Five warehouse he'd sold to the Public Health Service doctor who'd been so snotty to him in Galveston. The batch he'd ordered cut in half, then dyed with chemicals to disguise the difference in color.

"You think you're dealing with one of your southern-fried, ass-kissing Uncle Toms, Hogson? You know damn well what I'm talking about. Five hundred cases. Kids and old ladies dying because of you. You'll pay, Hogson. Believe me, you'll pay, before I'm through with you."

Hogson extended his hands in a pleading gesture. "Look, we can make a deal," he whined. "What's done is done. I could make you rich for life. You ever seen a hundred-thousand dollars? Or fifty? Or even ten?"

"Hogson, let me tell you something. I ain't here strictly for money. That's a fringe benefit. I'm here for you. Whether you keep breathin'—for now—is up to you."

"What the hell you really want, boy?" Hogson screamed, fear in his eyes.

Cole strode close, jammed the muzzle of the .45 under Hogson's chin. "Let's get one thing straight up front. I'd just as soon waste you as step on a cockroach, so don't think about playin' no games. Okay, I'll lay it on the line. First, you handwrite an order releasing a thousand cases of penicillin, good stuff, uncut I mean, from your warehouse. Second, a truck to haul it in. After that, we can talk about bread. For my time, and for the suffering you spread around at Camp Conolly."

"Sure, sure, anything," Hogson babbled, saliva dribbling from his mouth, running down his jaw. "You can have your goddamn penicillin. And the truck."

"Oh, and that ain't all, man," said Cole ominously.

"You mean there's more?"

"Didn't I just say so? A signed confession you sold that lousy, no-good garbage to the United States government. Kind of a guarantee I'll hold"—Cole laid the barrel of the Colt, not gently, across Hogson's temple, dropping him writhing on the rug—"that you won't pull none of this sleazy shit again, man. If I decided not to kill you, that is. You dig?"

Hogson indeed dug. Blood oozing from the side of his head, he hastened to comply.

Cole glanced at the documents bearing Hogson's wavering signature, folded them, stuffed them into his pocket.

"Now, you disgusting, fat prick," he said, "for some of my favorite color—green. Get it up. All of it."

Hogson's spirits temporarily lifted. Perhaps, he thought, he'd misread the situation after all. He was still alive, the Nigra had what he'd come for. Or at least most of it. The rest lay in the wall safe. Along with the Magnum.

"Upstairs," Cole said, prodding Hogson in the spine with the .45. On the way, they passed the sticky maroon stain where Hogson's head had hit the carpet. Lord, let me get my hands on that weapon, Hogson prayed silently. I need an equalizer. And that fabric I bled on cost me forty-five bucks a square yard.

With Cole breathing hard down the back of his neck, Hogson swung aside the Matisse he'd bought at auction in a Paris art gallery, revealing the recessed dial and circular door of the safe. With trembling fingers, he worked the combination. Opened it. Reached in. Felt the comforting solidity of the Magnum's butt. Played it cool. Waited for a better opportunity, when his visitor's attention might be diverted. Started passing stacks of currency back.

"Nine. Ten. Eleven. Twelve thousand. That's all there

is." Hogson's hand remained inside the safe, while his heart thumped noisily in his chest.

Cole's gaze strayed to the neat packages of hundred-dollar bills. The bastard's right, he thought. This *is* more bread than I've ever seen at one time before. But what the hell, it. . . .

Screwing up his courage, Hogson acted. Grasping the revolver, he dragged it from the safe, whirled with surprising speed for a man of his bulk, and blasted off a shot. The circumstance that forced Hogson to fire blindly, without really aiming, as he turned, saved Cole's life.

At that, the slug tore a half-inch-deep furrow along the upper portion of Cole's left arm, drove him off balance. Seizing his advantage, Hogson steadied his gun hand with the other and started to squeeze off a second round.

The .357 jammed.

Wild-eyed, sweating, Hogson desperately exerted pressure against a trigger which refused to budge. Across a distance of several feet, the two adversaries glared at each other.

Alonzo Cole said, "Glad you found that piece, Hogson. Sort of makes it self-defense, in my book."

The Colt bucked in Cole's fist. The first bullet caught Hogson squarely in the middle of his protruding belly. He dropped to his knees below the safe, screaming, pleading, cursing, hands clawing at the hole in his gut.

"No matter what gives with the bees, this old world's gonna be a better place with you out of it," Cole yelled. "That was just for openers." He walked over to Hogson and deliberately emptied the entire nine-shot clip into his body.

"Never done nothin' turned me on more since the first VC I zapped in 'Nam," he muttered.

Cole bandaged his wounded arm as best he could with a sleeve torn from one of the late Howard Hogson's custommade shirts, then left the Highland Park house in search of the warehouse. It was growing late, and he wasn't exactly familiar with Dallas streets.

In the early daylight hours of August 4, having floored the gas pedal of the heavily laden tractor-trailer most of the way, Alonzo Cole reached a deserted road junction between Alpine and Camp Connolly. A stand of scrubby trees, extending some distance back from the highway, dominated its southwest quadrant. Exhausted from pushing the big rig all night, his arm a throbbing hunk of pain where Hogson's bullet had gouged it, Cole failed to see the grisly fruit the oaks bore until he was nearly abreast of them.

Two naked corpses hung from the lower branches, swaying in the light breeze. Slowing the truck, Cole studied the bloated features above the ropes.

A gaunt, youngish man, heavily bearded, faces disfigured by a jagged scar. A plump, ripe-breasted girl who'd been Mexican or Spanish in life, by the look of her. Their executioners had appended explanatory signs. One read: "TEXAS JUSTICE FROM THE VIGILANTES. DEATH TO ALL FALSE PROPHETS." The second, apparently as an afterthought: "AND THEIR WHORES."

Picking up speed again, Cole speculated on the identity of the unfortunate pair and the crimes they might have committed to end up in this fashion.

At length, he shrugged. After all, death was no stranger to him. And victims of lynch mobs were commonplace sights in the United States these days.

"Dr. Messick, wake up."

Like many medical people, Laura possessed the happy faculty of being able to make the instant transition from deep sleep to almost full awareness. She did so now, despite the fact it was the first time her head had touched a pillow in over forty hours. Patty Barton, one of the floor nurses, stood near the head of her bed.

"There's a man outside, asking for you, Doctor," Patty said. "Asking for you. Says he has a truckload of penicillin to deliver."

Laura sat bolt upright, wondering if she'd heard correctly. "Penicillin? What penicillin? Dr. Klein told me not to expect any more."

"I don't know, Doctor. I'm only relaying a message."

Outside, Laura encountered Alonzo Cole. He stepped down from the cab of the tractor-trailer, banging the door shut behind him. Laura sensed there was something familiar about him. Then she remembered. He was the person who had inquired for Timmy Benjamin, sought to learn his condition several days, possibly a week or more, earlier.

"I don't understand at all, Mr.—ah—"

"Cole. Alonzo Cole."

"Mr. Cole. Where did this shipment come from?"

The ex-Viet Nam GI considered a moment, reaching for some rational explanation. He'd never worried about concocting a cover story for Dr. Messick. When he'd left for Dallas to run Hogson to earth, his actions had been strictly on a spur-of-the-moment basis, and still were. At last, inspiration arrived.

"Let's just say, Doc, these thousand cases of penicillin, undiluted by the way, are a gift from Howard Hogson. It took a little persuasion, but he finally saw the light."

Laura Messick stared from the truck to Cole, grasped partially the significance of the bloody shirt sleeve girding his left arm. Intuitively, she filled in some of the blanks, guessed the rest of the story. If Hogson were indeed dead, as she suspected, her immediate reaction was good riddance to bad rubbish. At least he'd left a legacy.

A legacy of life for her patients.

August 4, 1977

Despite confusion and bitterness, outraged grumblings directed toward Washington, and a firm conviction its elected officials hadn't the faintest idea what they were doing, the nation prepared to follow instructions and go underground.

The President was filmed and photographed turning the first spadeful of soil on the East Lawn of the White

House for a symbolic "First Family Shelter." If necessary, said Press Secretary Will Finlay, the President himself, the Cabinet, the Joint Chiefs of Staff, and key personnel vital to the orderly continuity of government would conduct the affairs of state from a SAC bomber somewhere over the United States.

As in almost every other phase of daily life since the bee threat had materialized on the horizon, heroes and villains abounded. Some made sacrifices, many aided crippled or elderly neighbors. A minority merely profited handsomely, or, like the parasites they were, attempted to claim-jump shelters already constructed by more industrious folk.

Across the land, dozens of citizens died from heart seizures and heat exhaustion incurred while digging. In Duluth, Minnesota, a Boy Scout troop gained momentary headlines by adopting as their current project completion of a subterranean installation for a geriatric nursing home. In Biloxi, Mississippi, whites and blacks alike toiled side by side, putting together a municipal shelter large enough to hold the entire population of the city. In Athens, Ohio, the town's wealthiest inhabitant donated several acres, lumber, concrete, and the labor of his construction firm employees. In Tucson, Arizona, members of all the craft unions volunteered their services without pay for the duration of the emergency.

Examples of less exemplary conduct emerged also. In Waterloo, Iowa, shovels sold at fifty dollars apiece. In Valverde, Texas, bulldozer owners demanded, and received, up to a thousand dollars a day for rental of their heavy equipment. Truckloads of canned goods and bottled water were hijacked daily on hundreds of highways, their contents later hawked at premium prices to those wishing to stock their shelters with nonperishable, emergency rations. An accountant in Bradenton, Florida, fatally shot his best friend in a dispute over a common bunker they had agreed to build on their adjoining properties.

So it went throughout the country. America, which had survived previous wars, famines, pestilences and floods, awaited yet another disaster of a frightening new dimension.

The bees, now cruising along in Central Mexico.

August 7, 1977

Minute by minute, hour by hour, anxiety and tension built up in Roy Ramsdell, until he felt like a boiler with a faulty emergency valve. He was, in short, on the point of explosion, the gauge needle of his sanity just short of the red "DANGER" area.

He'd experienced pressure before, working on projects, racing deadlines, supervising complicated research. But never before had the outcome of anything been so important, the need for a solution so vital, and, as he saw it, his own inadequacy so pitifully apparent. The cool scientific aplomb on which he'd always relied had deserted him completely of late. Besides, two weeks had elapsed since he'd seen Laura, with only a couple of hasty phone calls to ease the misery of separation. He told himself he must get away, if only for an hour or two, or risk going around the bend altogether.

Thus rationalizing what he had made up his mind to do in any event, Ramsdell said, "To hell with it, if anything breaks they know where to find me," hopped in his jeep and tore off in the direction of Camp Connolly.

"Roy!" Laura cried, her face radiant. "I tried to reach you, but you'd already left. I have. . . ."

Ramsdell halted further conversation through the simple, effective expedient of kissing her fervently. For the next several seconds they clung together, the dark world outside and the bees a million miles away. Ramsdell felt some of his troubles start to melt.

"What I started to tell you, dear heart, before I was so beautifully interrupted," Laura said, a smile on her drawn face, "was that I have some wonderful news."

"That I can sure stand. I'm afraid it's been in pretty short supply lately."

Laura proceeded to fill Ramsdell in on the miracle of the truckload of penicillin Alonzo Cole had procured in Dallas, the recovery of 99 percent of the pneumonia victims, the fact Timmy Benjamin was out of danger at last and asking for Ramsdell.

His brows arched. "The boy wants to see me? Whatever for? We've never even met. He doesn't know me, except possibly through you, nor I him. I can't see. . . ."

"You will, Roy. He told me he might have come up with an idea for stopping the bees from entering the United States."

Timmy seemed thin and worn, only to be expected, thought Ramsdell, from the ordeal he'd recently undergone. No doubt the natural resiliency of a healthy, thirteen-year old had helped to pull him through; that, plus a plentiful supply of full-strength penicillin.

"Roy Ramsdell," Laura was saying, making a smiling ceremony of the introduction, "This is Timmy Benjamin."

"Pleased to meet you, sir," Timmy said formally, extending his hand.

"Same here," Ramsdell said. "I've heard quite a lot about you. Dr. Messick's opinion is good enough for me. And before we go any farther, do me a favor and dispense with the 'sir,' okay? I appreciate the courtesy, but it makes me feel uncomfortable. And old, I might add. Why not try 'Roy' on for size?"

Timmy grinned. "My parents always taught me to obey my elders. Roy it is."

"Dr. Messick said you'd worked out a possible defense against those obscene flying objects south of the border."

"She's right, Roy. I might have. Then again, it may be nothing. You'll have to be the judge of that. Here, take a look."

Timmy reached under the bedcovers, pulled out a tattered, dogeared magazine, extended it to Ramsdell.

"Read the advertisement, Roy, on the left side of page eighty," said Timmy.

Ramsdell noted it was a *Sports Illustrated* from Sep-

tember, 1974, nearly three years previous. He frowned.
Nobody was worrying about bees then. No one had yet
heard of *apis mellifera adansonii*. Could the kid have
been pulling Laura's leg? he wondered. And his? If so,
Timmy's timing was atrocious, his sense of humor worse.
Ramsdell glanced sharply at the youngster, noted the
hopeful, alert, anticipatory brown eyes, and decided he'd
been way off base. Obviously, Timmy Benjamin was
deadly serious in his belief he'd found a way to help.

Ramsdell leafed through the pages until he arrived at
the ad the boy had indicated.

Laura stood at his elbow, peering over his shoulder.
"I'm afraid when these camps were on the drawing board,
none of the planners thought to include provisions for
up-to-date reading material."

"Don't apologize," Ramsdell said. "You visited a den-
tist's office lately? You're lucky if they give you anything
newer than *Liberty* or *Godey's Ladies' Book*."

The ad turned out to be a slick, four-color job for a
multinational company whose name Ramsdell recognized
instantly. For some years, the firm's major public accept-
ance and profitability had derived from the field of per-
ishable foodstuffs. They sent expensive items such as
prime strip steaks, filets mignons, lobsters, jumbo shrimp,
and Florida stone crabs to a far-flung coterie of customers
in the four corners of the globe. Frozen solid, packed in
dry ice, rushed by jet, orders arrived almost as soon as
the client had sent his letter or made his telephone call.
The company's trademark was a winged Black Angus
Bull, with the logo underneath, "WE SHIP ANY-
WHERE: OVER THE STATE LINE, OR OVER THE
SEA."

Ramsdell smiled, conjuring up a vision of a charbroiled
sirloin or porterhouse, inch-and-a-half thick, medium
rare. The memory was all that remained. He hadn't seen
either in months now.

"This is all very interesting, Timmy, but frankly I fail
to see the connection. Bees? Beefsteaks? For heaven's
sake, let me in on the secret."

"Bear with me a minute, Roy. I will. Ever since my

parents were killed, nearly four months ago, I tried to learn every detail I could about bees. I read whatever material was available. I asked questions of people who'd been stung and lived through it, as I did. Dr. Messick explained to me maybe I was curious about bees because of Mom and Dad. I don't know. Before that happened, I guess I never really cared one way or another. Bees were just . . . there. You know what I mean, a part of nature, like butterflies or frogs. Anyway, isn't it true, Roy, that bees hibernate during the winter?"

Ramsdell considered a moment. "Of course. They have to. They're cold-blooded creatures. They cluster in cold weather for warmth, keep the interior of their hives like a steam bath, ninety-five or a hundred degrees. If the external temperature plunged to, say, twenty degrees, and the bees ventured outside, within minutes they'd drop dead, one by one. At least that's the opinion of my esteemed associate, Henry Maddox. Fine. Great. But Timmy, where are you going to find any winter in the midst of the . . . hottest . . . summer . . . the . . ."

Ramsdell's speech ran down, an old clock somebody had neglected to wind. His mouth hung open. He stared at Timmy Benjamin in unabashed admiration, as the blinding bulb of truth suddenly flashed on inside his head.

"Unless you created an artificial climate, turned summer into winter," said Timmy. His matter-of-fact, low-key statement made it into a simple process, performed routinely every day of the week and twice on Sundays.

Ramsdell's brain slipped into gear, raced off in several different directions at a high rate of speed. He examined the proposition from all angles. Reviewed stored information pertaining to climatology, the science of weather and weather patterns. Dwelled upon refrigeration agents and their physical properties, such as Freon and the fluorinated hydrocarbons, ammonia, solid carbon dioxide, or dry ice as it was more commonly known. Tossed in snow-making machines of the size and capacity in use at ski resorts. Shot theoretical cryogenic bullets into clouds laden with moist, humid air to produce freezing precipitation, in the same manner that silver iodide particle seeding will sometimes bring rain down on a drought-stricken area. Weighed the whole equation in the balance, estimated its feasibility level at 30 percent, even dared to hope again. He agreed the three-in-ten odds could be higher; still, Timmy's brainstorm, he figured, lay within the realm of possibility.

Abruptly sitting down on the bed, Ramsdell gathered Timmy into his arms, hugged him joyfully, nearly smothered him until Laura came to the rescue. Then Ramsdell embraced her, too, bestowing his restored good spirits on both impartially. Simultaneously, he began to laugh, great gusts shaking him, tears glistening on his cheeks.

Laura said, "Roy Ramsdell, you're some piece of work! The situation the country's in is about as humorous as an autopsy report. You ought to be ashamed of yourself."

"Yeah, Roy," Timmy chimed in. "Did I say something all *that* funny?"

Ramsdell shook his head, wiped his eyes, and regained a measure of sobriety. "No, of course not, Timmy. It's just that for months the finest scientific minds in the world have been struggling with this bee problem and getting nowhere. Out of a clear, blue sky a thirteen-year-old boy with a two-year-old magazine makes us all look like idiots, yours truly and his alleged superior intelligence included. Funny? Not really. Brilliant. Utterly, completely brilliant. With a good chance of proving effective. Which is more than I can say for some of the gems I've come up with in the past."

Ramsdell sobered momentarily, remembering (could he ever forget?) the disaster at the Panama Canal Zone.

Optimism, he chided himself. The power of positive thinking. Timmy's scheme *must* not fail, *would* not fail, though it involved utilization of a little-known scientific discipline, the quick exploitation of a technology not yet totally developed.

To state the facts bluntly, it represented the last chance for the United States. And perhaps all mankind.

August 8, 1977

Alonzo Cole had received four Purple Hearts in Viet Nam. He therefore considered himself somewhat of an expert on the subject of gunshot wounds, superficial and serious.

Thus, from past experience, he expected his left arm to stay painful for at least forty-eight hours, which it did. After that, he looked forward to its spontaneous healing, which it did not. By the third day, it had begun to swell instead, with angry, reddened streaks radiating in all directions. On the fourth, obviously badly infected, the furrow inflicted by Hogson's .357 had become one large, compounded agony. Frightened, he realized then he'd been a fool to neglect the injury, and sought out Dr. Messick without further delay.

She instantly diagnosed the cause of the wound, cleaned and dressed it, gave him a quarter-grain of morphine for pain, a tetanus shot, antibiotics, and a savage lecture.

"Didn't it ever occur to you the bullet might have driven cloth fragments from your jacket into the flesh?" she asked. "And that eventually your arm could suppurate?"

"Do what?"

"Get infected. Discharge pus. This is an awful mess, Mr. Cole. Why did you let it go so long?"

He shrugged. "What the hell, Doc, I never had no trouble before. Always healed fast and clean when I was in 'Nam. Shrapnel twice, machine gun slugs two other times. I'm hard to kill, I guess."

"Immediate medical attention under sterile conditions makes a great deal of difference, you know."

She fell silent, studying the clusters of puncture holes in the mahogany-colored skin of both arms that she'd noted at the beginning of her examination. Obviously, the man had been a drug addict. But, she could see, he was no more; the needle tracks were indistinct, scarred over. She felt a sudden surge of respect, even admiration for Cole, who had risked so much, laid his life on the line to liberate penicillin from Howard Hogson and bring it to Camp Connolly. On several occasions, Laura had seen people like Cole wrestling with the private hell of detoxification. It wasn't a pleasant sight. She determined on the spot not to pry, since the details of Cole's past really didn't concern her, professionally or otherwise.

At the same time, Alonzo Cole's thoughts were racing. Since his return from Dallas, the tiny acorn of an idea had implanted itself in his mind, grown, and finally burst into full bloom. While the concept possessed the dual merits of simplicity and workability, Cole suspiciously questioned his motivations. Why should he all of a sudden worry about the welfare of others, he wondered, when no one had ever given a rat's ass about him? Why the startling reversal of character, concerning himself with the future, in place of living from one day to the next as he'd always done? Then, too, he had neither the education nor the medical knowledge to iron out the possible bugs on his own. Besides, he foresaw additional complicating factors—the civil authorities, such as they'd become, and the Army Military Police. In short, Cole wanted help, yet feared to ask for it. Unbidden, all the old suspicion and distrust rose to the surface. Could he open up to this white woman, and if so, how far? For a moment he wavered, finally decided to take the plunge.

"Doc, tell me straight out," he said. "Suppose I was to lay a few hard facts on you. About things I done. Ugly. Illegal. Criminal. I heard once somewhere you'd have to keep quiet about 'em, couldn't spill 'em to nobody because you're a doctor. That true?"

She nodded. "Of course, Mr. Cole. It's a vital part of the Hippocratic Oath we all swear to and agree to uphold. The physician-patient relationship. Whatever you choose to say to me I am bound to keep in strictest confidence. I can't be forced to reveal it even under oath in court. Same as an attorney and a client. Or a priest in the confessional."

Reassured, Cole said, "Okay, if that's the way it is. Doc, I'm no dope and neither are you. I seen you eyeballing my arms a while ago. You know what the score is. I used to be a junkie, was for years until I kicked accidentally, while I was mostly out of my head for a week. Idea came to me, if it worked good for me, why not others? Black, white, brown, what the hell's the difference? Put 'em under somehow, keep 'em under long enough to kick easier. For sure methadone ain't been the answer, not the way I hear it. I s'pose what I'm trying to say is, I'd like to set up a clinic. Open to all races. Where don't matter. If the first one does its job, there could be more. I'd want to get personally involved, maybe hold rap sessions, convince the poor hype bastards if I can shed a hundred-dollar-a-day habit, they can too. Look, Doc, I got no training, no trade, not a damn thing I'm able to earn a livin' with outside the Army. That I tried already, and it's no dice. This is the only road I've figured out to take to do something with my life. Only I don't know nothing about gettin' started, who to go to, I mean, or if they'd bother listening. You dig me?"

Laura peered directly into Cole's eyes and saw suffering, hurt, and doubt reflected there. She sympathized with him, realizing the amount of courage required for an individual of Cole's background to unburden himself even this much.

"Yes, I understand," she said softly. "My first reaction is to stand up and applaud. Frankly, Mr. Cole, I think it's a wonderful, well-conceived idea. Of course I'd be willing to lend a hand. You can stop worrying about the nuts and bolts. They'll all fall into place by themselves one day. So it's settled."

"No, not really, Doc," said Cole. "Not by a long shot. I'm glad you said what you did, eases my mind some, but that's only a part of my problem. Hell, I guess we're just sittin' here jivin' each other, because there ain't no way this is ever gonna happen. Not when seventeen different kinds of fuzz want a piece of my hide."

Then the floodgates really swung wide, and Cole bared his soul. The words poured forth in a steady torrent, a dam shattering its concrete prison, waters from a raging river overflowing the banks. Cole simply let it all hang out to Laura.

Hogson, and how the shady wheeler-dealer had died. Lieutenant Pak. The officers in Viet Nam. His desertion from the armed forces. The mugging, robbery, and assault episodes of his Times Square days. The entire sordid history, omitting nothing, glossing over nothing. Finished, he hung his head.

"So you see, Doc," he said, "I gotta forget the whole deal. Minute I'd get into it, the pigs'd come swarmin' around. If I ever saw daylight again, I'd be a hundred-and-ten-years old. I been in civilian slammers and military stockades too. I can't do no more time. That's it. Period."

"Not even if it meant wiping the slate clean forever? Serving a relatively short stretch?" Laura had been sincere in extending her offer of assistance. In her mind's eye, she envisioned an out for Cole, the vague glimmerings of a possible solution. It would require his cooperation, and that of Roy Ramsdell. She made no judgments, evaluated from her heart rather than from her head. In the final analysis, she considered Alonzo Cole a man worth saving and transforming into a useful, productive citizen. "Giving yourself up might be the first step in the right direction," she said.

Cole laughed, forgetting the pain in his arm momentarily. "You kiddin,' Doc? You think I'd live long enough to stand trial in Texas for icing Hogson? Me, a black man? Hell, no. The vigilantes are hangin' honkies out there even. Then there's the matter of the time I owe the Army and New York City. Sorry, Doc. No way. It just wouldn't work."

"Not even if Roy Ramsdell went to bat for you with the highest authority?" she said. "And I mean the highest. The President of the United States."

"Your friend Ramsdell'd talk to the President 'bout taking me off the hook? He don't owe me nothin.' Why should he?"

"Because I told him how many hundreds of lives you saved by squeezing that penicillin out of Hogson. It's something the law calls 'mitigating circumstances.' And remember, Hogson shot you first. You didn't kill the man in cold blood, much as he merited it. By the same token, the President is Commander-in-Chief of the Armed Forces. I'm sure Roy might be able to persuade him to wipe the AWOL business off the books. He has the power. Didn't President Nixon intervene for Lieutenant Calley?"

"Yeah, sure, but—Christ, Doc, I don't know, I just don't know. I'd be taking a hell of a chance, 'less somebody gave me some solid guarantees. Sure have to think hard about it. Long and hard.

"Then, too, there's Timmy to consider, Doc. That's one hell of a kid. Whatever we've got goin' between us is like no other emotion I ever felt in my life before. Hard to put my finger on it, y'know, but it's there. He's got guts and he's been hurt bad, same as me, I s'pose. I'd hate for him to find out about my past. Maybe then he wouldn't like me no more. So you see, there ain't only me to consider. Like I said, it'll take thinkin' on. And I don't expect to come up with an answer in the next ten minutes, either."

"Good enough, Cole," she said. "In the meantime, I'll speak to Roy. In my opinion, you deserve a break. I intend to see you get it. You have my word on that."

Departing with his arm cleansed and bandaged, but still throbbing, Cole mumbled thanks to Laura. His brain was in a ferment, torn between conflicting desires. Life had taught him early one couldn't usually have it both ways, that every pleasure was linked with an accompanying pain.

He sighed. No matter what, he'd do exactly as he'd promised Dr. Messick. Think it over, long and hard.

October 18, 1977

WILL SUPERSECRET WEATHER PROJECT PROVE FINAL SOLUTION TO BEE THREAT?

By Edward Edelson, Science Editor, *New York Daily News*

Sanderson, Texas, Oct. 17—"Billions of dollars have been poured into 'Project Cold Front', and further billions no doubt will be, in the most concerted government effort yet to bar the entry of swarming hordes of killer bees into the United States from Mexico.

"Never since World War II has security been so tight, factual news at such a premium. A great deal of the unprecedented activity unfolding around the periphery of this border town is highly classified. Apparently it is destined to remain so. Attempts by print and electronic journalists to pierce the veil of secrecy are met with either silence or brusque orders to move on.

"Rendering normal reportage double difficult is the edict barring newsmen from entering a ten-mile-wide zone on the American side of the Rio Grande River. Several weeks ago, when he announced first bare details of 'Project Cold Front,' the President defended creation of the so-called 'no man's land' as necessary from a security standpoint to forestall possible espionage and to allow unhindered access to the area by workers and equipment. Along the entire winding 700-mile length of the river, from the Gulf to the New Mexico state line, a barbed-wire barricade seals off entry to press and public alike. Searchlights play on the wire at night. Armed guards with ferocious dogs patrol it twenty-four hours a day.

"Routine handouts from government public relations men are vague and bare of detail. However, from questioning of usually reliable sources who prefer not to be quoted, plus the meager amount of personal observation permitted, the following picture of 'Project Cold Front' emerges:

"In the past five weeks, hundreds of miles of pipe have been laid in the vicinity of the Rio Grande. Their exact location and disposition are both classified items, but they carry refrigeration agents in liquid form. All commercial manufacturers of solid carbon dioxide, or dry ice, are in production on a wartime footing, under direct government control, with sales to civilians expressly prohibited. Snow-making machines from the ski slopes of California, Colorado, the northern tier of states, and New England has been requisitioned and brought here.

"In addition (and this is where security becomes especially sensitive), it was learned that SECT, the Special Environmental Control Team engaged in weather change research for the military over the last several years, is based here and is part of the overall effort. While their installation is visible from behind the barbed wire, no hint of their specific role has leaked out.

"Finally, the United States recently sent aloft into the troposphere and ionosphere several Orbital Climate Control Satellites, nicknamed 'Orbies' by NASA. Again, their exact function and operational data are closely guarded secrets. All that is definitely known of the 'Orbies' is that they influence change in upper air patterns by some means.

"On a joint inspection tour today, both the President and Roy Ramsdell, head of the Irregulars group, provided few answers for reporters. Cautiously, they confirmed that water temperature of the Rio Grande itself, and air temperatures along its length, are dropping at a satisfactory rate. They declined comment on figures, as well as the ultimate level to which the thermometer must plunge if the bees are to be confronted with a Hobson's choice: die or turn back.

"As usual honest and candid during the interviews with the press, Ramsdell said he could take credit for neither the original idea for, nor the innovative techniques embodied in, 'Project Cold Front'. The former, according to Ramsdell, rightfully belongs to thirteen-year-old Timothy Benjamin. The youngster will be remembered for his harrowing amateur radio broadcast of the Costa Rican bee attack that took the lives of his parents last April 18. The latter, said Ramsdell, is thanks to the knowledgeable meteorology and climatology specialists he had added to his group over the past two and a half months.

"According to the latest projections, if the billions of bees now in Mexico continue progressing at their present speed, and on their present course, they will reach the Rio Grande in the vicinity of Sanderson between November 15 and November 20.

"Notwithstanding tight security, high-level secrecy, barbed wire, the presence of machine-gun toting armed guards, and the sparseness of real information, the conviction grows that hope is the keynote of this massive enterprise. Discreetly expressed, perhaps, but still genuine hope."

November 17, 1977

At 3:18 P.M., news of the imminent approach of the swarm was relayed by radio from Kent Grayson, patrolling in a helicopter several miles south on the Mexican side of the Rio Grande, to Ramsdell, Maddox and the rest of the "Irregulars" in their underground observation post behind the river on Texas soil.

"They're just coming into view, Roy", Grayson shouted into his mike. "Looks like a solid black rectangle, five hundred to a thousand feet high, stretching maybe ten miles back toward the horizon. Jesus Christ, it's an incredible sight! This many bees airborne, I mean. In Mexico City, they were resting on the ground, remember?"

"You bet I do, Kent. And that's where I wish they were now. Only dead. What's their exact compass heading?"

"325° true. At their present speed, they should reach your position before nightfall. As they used to say in the Japanese Navy, buddy, rotsa ruck."

"And then some. Stay above 'em, Kent, and keep tracking. Let me know immediately if they change course."

"Will do, Roy. Over and out."

Henry Maddox turned to Ramsdell, his face grave inside the furred circle of the arctic parka he was wearing. "Well, here we go again," he said. "Canal Zone Two, on instant replay. Or something like."

"Yeah. Except there, we were sweating our butts off. Now, we're freezing them off. It's a welcome change, I must say. What's the external temperature in our zone? Have you checked it in the last hour?"

"Still 31° Fahrenheit, Roy. No matter how hard we try, we can't take it any lower. Frankly, I think it's a miracle we've come this far, considering how long the rotten heat's hung around. The Orbies helped a hell of a lot. So did the piped refrigerants and the dry ice. Snow blowers weren't powerful enough to have much effect, and the cryogenic cloud seeding turned out to be a flop. We'll have to put that one back on the drawing board."

"Well, we can talk until we're blue in the face, Henry, but in the final analysis there's only one criterion. Will the cold barrier kill *these* bees as well as it did in our operational tests?"

Maddox shrugged. "Hard to say. Theoretically, yes. Don't forget our test subjects were all plain old *Apis mellifera,* domestic German and Italian bees. No Africans, no hybrids, no mutants. Anyway, I'd sure be happier if we could have brought the readings at least into the middle twenties. Remember, we stunned a lot of the test bees, too, which means we should be able to dispose of the ones we don't kill outright on the ground. Don't forget, Roy, we have one valuable plus going for us. None of the swarm on its way here is programmed for winter. In the first place, they haven't met up with any yet. Then, too, they've been travelling too fast to have learned the techniques of 'hiving up'—sealing off their hives, stockpiling honey, and so forth—even if they'd needed them. So, separating fact from pure optimism, I still think we have a pretty good shot."

"Let's hope so, for all our sakes. Just look outside, will you? Isn't that something?"

The two men, scientific researcher and entomologist, gazed in unison at a bleak, desolate scene that might have been lifted unchanged from a Lunar or Martian landscape. The metamorphosis they had brought about in establishing "Project Cold Front" was indeed startling.

Trees, cactus plants, scrub growth all lay withered, sere, shrivelled, blasted by the sudden precipitate drop in the normal steel-mill furnace temperatures. Piles of once-frozen slush had half-melted to form rime-rimmed troughs of gooey, brown mud. The Rio Grande itself, historical border crossing point for illegal wetbacks, outlaws, adventurers and on occasion legitimate travellers, was wreathed in a chill, smoky mist. Tendrils of fog twisted upward from the dirty waters, concrete proof of heroic efforts by the Orbiting Weather Satellites and the Special Environmental Control Teams in creating the belt of artificial cold.

Hourly reports drifted in from Kent Grayson in the tracking chopper. Tension mounted to unbearable heights among Maddox, Ramsdell, Barney Lippert, other members of the "Irregulars" group, the SECT teams, government observers, warmly-clad technicians whose work required them to remain at posts in the barbed-wire-enclosed "no man's land" strip.

Finally, the waiting ended. As Grayson had predicted, just before sunset the vanguard of the enormous phalanx of bees neared, for the first time in their northward migration, the United States proper.

Grayson's voice boomed again from the speaker. "I'm right on top of the main body, Roy. Far enough above to keep it all in view."

"Yes, we have you in visual contact from here. How's it look?"

"Bigger than Mexico, I'd guess. Talk about Robert Ripley and his Marching Chinese! Well, the rest is up to you science types. They're flying in toward you, at about ten o'clock high. Need me for anything else?"

"Negative. You can pack it in if you want."

Grayson chuckled. "If you don't mind, I think I'll stay aloft for a while. This is one mission I'd just as soon not work at ground level."

"Suit yourself. *Ciao*, for now."

The leading scout elements winged in, heading directly for the belt of cold that started at the Mexican shoreline. They entered it at full speed, furry bodies reflected in the reddish glow of the sinking sun. Slowed, as the lowered temperatures jolted their senses, disturbed their metabolic processes. They dipped and yawed erratically, clawed for altitude, then died, or became comatose. Bees fluttered in multi-colored myriads down to the river's surface. Floated there for a space, to be joined by increasing numbers of their comrades. Some of the larger, older specimens managed to survive long enough to perish in the shallows on the American side, or even on Texas soil itself. But perish they did, by the thousands and millions and hundreds of millions, as windrows of bee corpses piled up over an ever-widening area.

On the point of wrapping each other in a bear hug and breaking into an impromptu victory dance, Maddox and Ramsdell simultaneously spied a chilling tableau.

"Henry!" Ramsdell shouted. "Up there. To your right, between two and three o'clock. Put the binoculars on that bunch halfway across the water."

Maddox did so, and the view was blood curdling.

Wings beating steadily, making tangible headway against the barriers that had taken the lives of so many of their swarm mates, a squadron of the huge orange-and-black *adansonii* gained the Texas shore of the Rio

Grande. Some fell in transit, others faltered in flight and slowed. A large percentage, however, continued on their way through the sub-freezing barrier apparently unharmed, at length disappearing from view to the northwest, a direction that would ultimately carry them to the vicinity of Alpine and DP camps.

Maddox lowered the field glasses, slumped over in horror. "Unbelievable!" he whispered, his words so low Ramsdell had to strain to catch them. "We dropped the temperature enough so we're killing or stunning the ordinary *Apis mellifera*, but not the *adansonii*, goddam it! Can nothing kill it? We knew about its increased flight range. Super size. The mass intelligence we confirmed at the Canal Zone. And now, after all else. . . ." Maddox fell silent, fists clenched, staring straight ahead as if personally locking eyes with a renewed spectre of defeat.

"Hardiness and physical stamina even we never suspected," Ramsdell concluded the sentence Maddox had left dangling in midair.

Hour after hour, until well past midnight, the glare of floodlights revealed the same shocking spectacle.

Grudgingly, the gigantic bee mass disintegrated. Was slaughtered outright as it attempted to force its way through the climatic trap, or corkscrewed groundward, stunned, to be finished off by flamethrowers and jellied napalm. Turned back in disoriented confusion toward Mexico. Seeking escape, veered east and west, away from the Sanderson area, fell prey to the cold at McNary and El Paso and Del Rio and Eagle Pass.

But their strength and numbers nearly undiminished, countless columns of adansonii *hybrids survived, passing over the river, fanning out into south central Texas.*

A distraught Ramsdell refused to allow his mind to dwell on the terror, chaos, and panic that would ensue if the bees were allowed to menace the inhabitants of the overcrowded DP cities. All other considerations aside, he told himself, Laura Messick stood in their possible path too.

With a heavy heart, Ramsdell picked up the telephone,

prepared to call the President and brief him on the latest developments in The War Against The Bees.

He hated to heap additional burdens on such an already sorely troubled individual. How, he wondered, did one tell a lame duck Chief Executive, recently voted out of office by a disenchanted electorate, who just a few months before had "pledged his sacred honor" such an occurrence would never take place, that in truth it had? How explain, in seemingly contradictory terms, that they had won, yet at the same time lost?

November 18, 1977

The remainder of the sleepless night and half the day that followed, as Roy Ramsdell reviewed their events later, became a blurred montage of orders, decisions, mopping up, and renewed surveillance of the marauding insects that had eluded "Operation Cold Front."

With the bees broken up into small, disorganized, more manageable groups to the south, Mexican government officials and most of the Army and Air Force returned from their self-imposed exile, began conducting "search-and-destroy" missions to clean up isolated pockets left here and there.

Detailed reports received in a constant stream from SECT control stations along the 700-mile length of the Rio Grande conveyed essentially the same facts Maddox and Ramsdell had observed personally around Sanderson.

Apis mellifera largely destroyed or scattered at the river. *Adansonii* in significant numbers inland on the broad Texas plain.

Ramsdell sent a weary Kent Grayson aloft to pinpoint their location and keep tabs on their movement and activity, if any. In a bitter moment of candid evaluation, Ramsdell cursed the futility of the aerial reconnaissance. What difference did it make where the stupid bees were, he asked himself, when he didn't have the faintest idea how to dispose of them in any case?

"Got 'em, Roy," Grayson said over the CP receiver early in the afternoon. "Can't even estimate their numbers. If I said zillions I'd be in the ballpark."

"Where, Kent?" Ramsdell wanted to know. "And what're they doing?"

"One thing at a time. I've run up and down the Rio Grande, widening my sweep patterns, ever since dawn. They're farther to the north and east than I thought."

"Give me your present location."

"About ten miles southwest of Rocksprings, at the edge of Devils Lake, I've just returned from Bracketville and Uvalde. The damn fools were there. Here at the lake, too. Up north, at Sonora, and on the lower half of the Edwards Plateau. They're along the banks of the Pecos at McCamey. Next, I plan on swinging west, to take a little look-see around Fort Stockton and Fort Davis. As an educated guess, Roy, the bees are spread out over nine, ten-thousand square miles at least."

"I hope that was the bad news," Ramsdell groaned. "Is there anything for the lads in the white hats to cheer about?"

"Yeah, if you strain hard enough. They're stationary, not moving, just sitting, same as they did at Mexico City and in Costa Rica back in April."

"Well, that's a comfort. For the moment. Keep us posted."

Forty-five minutes later, Grayson was back on the horn, a puzzled note evident in his voice.

"Hey, you guys, there's something screwy going on. External temperature's dropped almost eight degrees since I talked to you last. The sky's darkening. And the wind's picking up pretty good from the north. Matter of fact, it's turbulent as hell up here. You getting the same readings at ground level?"

Ramsdell said, "Hold on, Kent. I'll check. We've been busy." He glanced over at Maddox, seeking confirmation of Grayson's report. "Henry says negative. Air temp's staying constant, meaning high nineties, outside the 'Operation Cold Front' sector. But affirmative on the wind velocity, except ours is from the south, twenty knots, gusting to thirty-five."

"Huh. Strange. I sure can't figure it out. Nor am I about to try, at this altitude. It appears our friends are bedded down for a while. I'm coming in."

"Roger, Kent. And forget the swing to the west. Set down before conditions worsen. You've done your job."

Ramsdell turned to Maddox. "You have any idea what's happening where Grayson is? Or why?"

The white-haired bee expert shook his head. "Hell, no. Should I, Roy? I'm no meteorologist. North winds. South winds. Maybe we disturbed something upstairs with the Orbies, the SECT teams, our efforts at climate control. Who knows?"

A short time later, Grayson contacted the base again. Where he had exhibited wonderment and uncertainty on the previous transmission, his current message contained a breathless, urgent note of excitement.

"Roy! Roy!" he shouted. "I've been monitoring the AM radio band, to pick up a weather advisory. I got more than I bargained for! It's on every station! I'm passing over Sanderson, listening to KSND. Reception's lousy, due to atmospheric conditions. But this much I can tell you, garbled or not. We're in for a blizzard, a real Ding-Dong-Daddy of a blizzard!"

"A *what*?" Ramsdell shot back. "Christ's sake, Kent, in the middle of a heat wave that's lasted two years? You got a bottle stashed in the cockpit?"

"Not really, skipper. But I wish I had! Give a listen yourself. You can probably hear it better down there."

Ramsdell wasted no time complying. He twisted the tuning dial to the 1410 kHz setting of KSND, waited impatiently until the announcer's voice blared forth in mid-sentence.

" . . . throughout the remainder of the day. Tonight, temperatures are expected to dip as low as zero to five above, with high winds of forty miles per hour gusting to sixty, causing the looked-for heavy snowfall to blow and drift in blizzard conditions. Travellers' warnings are posted for the five-state area of New Mexico, Texas,

Oklahoma, Arkansas, and Louisiana. On the basis of available information, weather forecasters project that the storm will concentrate its fury over the lower part of Texas, south of an imaginary line drawn from El Paso to Houston. Repeating this KSND weather advisory, a warning of. . . ."

Ramsdell snapped the radio off. While not a particularly religious person, he had long experienced something else—something greater—in his meditation. Now he was suddenly overwhelmed with the feeling that there was a higher power of some sort after all. Was it possible mankind was going to be gifted with the miracle Ramsdell had spoken of to Harvey Nettles, the Secretary of the Treasury, on that long-ago day in the White House?

"You heard the man, Henry," he said to Maddox.

"I did."

"And? What's the joker in the deck? Will this do what I think it should?"

"Kill the hybrids that survived, you mean? If these were run-of-the-mill bees, I'd say sure, unquestionably, with readings like that. But these *aren't*, Roy. No, indeed. We're dealing with *Apis mellifera adansonii*. The goddamn superbees that've mocked us and made assholes of us ever since we first laid eyes on 'em! Indestructible. Immortal. Impervious. You know something?"

"What?"

"I'll reserve judgement. Wait and see. Because I'm afraid to offer a prediction, my knowledge and my instinct conflicting as they do. And maybe I'll even pray to a Deity I don't believe in. Might just as well. I've tried everything else."

November 18-19, 1977

The swarm stirred, as it felt the initial whisper of wind from the north, became aware of slowly changing temperatures. Their alarm pheromones warned them of incipient danger, but as yet they could not divine its source. A curious few rose from the ground, probed experimentally at the new threat in the offing, coming as it did hard on the heels of their perilous passage through the belt of cold at the Rio Grande. They did not, however, remain airborne long, dropping back down again in a tired, listless fashion.

By degrees, the wind velocity accelerated, first to a whine, then a whistling roar, finally a numbing, fullblown hymn of hatred. As the wind became stronger, the mercury dropped at a corresponding rate. Thoroughly confused, uncertain as to what course to follow, the instinctive group intelligence of the *adansonii* bees told them retreat was in order, even though it meant a second passage through the arificial barrier at the river that had so sapped their collective strength. Fearful of this new dimension that had intruded itself into their existence, that was actually hurling them this way and that with its power, they zigzagged haphazardly into the air in all their infinite numbers, battered veterans of a military engagement for whom rest and recuperation had suddenly ended.

Turning south then, the swarm had proceeded but a short distance before a fresh disaster overtook them. Shrieking winds from that compass quadrant drove them back to their original starting point. Later, still seeking refuge from the howling vortex formed by the meeting of the northern and southern air flows, the bees found themselves confronted by the ultimate enemy—untold tons of snow pouring down upon them in a veritable hell of gale-driven flakes.

As the thermometer nosedived below the freezing mark, to twenty, to ten, to five degrees above zero, and the chill factor registered minus forty or fifty, the extraordinarily strong strain of bees bred initially by Warwick Kerr over two decades earlier began to die.

The tawny-furred killers' wings fluttered slowly to a halt, their bodily functions slowed, finally ceased altogether. Whirled about in the maelstrom of the storm, at the mercy of Force Seven Beaufort Scale blasts, their bodies littered the countryside. Black forms cascaded down, lifeless, on lake and river, mountain and plain, rock and soil, to be covered by a drifting coverlet of snow.

COPY OF A UNITED PRESS INTERNATIONAL DISPATCH MOVED ON THE FULL RADIO WIRE THROUGHOUT THE COUNTRY:

FOR AIRING ALL RADIO WIRE CLIENTS. BACKGROUND SIDE-BAR TO PREVIOUS WEATHER STORY. SPECIAL ATTENTION STATIONS IN NEW MEXICO, TEXAS, OKLAHOMA, ARKANSAS AND LOUISIANA. USE AT WILL.

"BY FRED ATKINS, UPI WASHINGTON

GOVERNMENT METEOROLOGISTS HERE AGREE THAT THE FREAK STORM CURRENTLY SLASHING ITS WAY THROUGH SOUTHWESTERN TIER AND GULF COAST STATES HAD ITS GENESIS IN THE VAGARIES OF THE JET STREAM. THIS COMPLICATED CURRENT, A SWIRLING WIND BELT SOME 40,000 FEET ABOVE THE EARTH'S SURFACE, FLUCTUATES AND DEVIATES THROUGHOUT THE ENTIRE YEAR, ESPECIALLY OVER NORTH AMERICA.

ON INFREQUENT OCCASIONS, PERHAPS TWICE A CENTURY, THE JET STREAM WILL BEND DRASTICALLY TO THE SOUTH. WHEN THIS PHENOMENON OCCURS, ACCORDING TO EDWARD SOKOLSKY, CHIEF U.S. WEATHER BUREAU METEOROLOGIST, THE JET STREAM MOVES ACROSS THE ROCKIES INTO OLD MEXICO, THEN SCOOPS NORTHEASTWARD THROUGH THE GULF OF MEXICO AND UP INTO THE APPALACHIANS.

"'FROM THE UNUSUAL BENDING OF THE JET STREAM SOUTH OF THE BORDER,' SOKOLSKY SAID, 'FRIGID ARCTIC AIR WAS ENABLED TO ROAR UNMOLESTED THROUGH CANADA, THE PLAINS STATES AND ON INTO TEXAS AND THE GULF AREA. THERE IT CLASHED WITH WARM, MOIST AIR SWEEPING UP FROM SOUTH AMERICA AND CENTRAL AMERICA AT HIGH SPEEDS, DUE TO EXTENSIVE FOREST AND JUNGLE DEFOLIATION IN THOSE REGIONS. THE COLLISION OF THE TWO EXTREMES—HEAT AND COLD—PRODUCED SEVERE SNOWSTORMS IN TEXAS AS FAR SOUTH AS BROWNSVILLE, IN LOUISIANA AND THREE ADJACENT STATES.'

"CONCLUDED SOKOLSKY, 'THE LAST RECORDED INSTANCE OF SUCH ABERRANT BEHAVIOR ON THE PART OF THE JET STREAM OCCURRED IN 1899, WHEN THE GREATEST PRIOR MODERN ARCTIC SPELL IN THE SOUTH OCCURRED. SO SEVERE

WERE WEATHER CONDITIONS THEN THAT AN ALL-TIME
LOW OF TWO DEGREES BELOW ZERO WAS NOTED IN FLOR-
IDA.'
"10:58 P 11/18 JL"

December 11, 1977

With much head-shaking and tongue-clucking on the
part of the industrious, once-a-week cleaning lady,
Mrs. Daly, Roy Ramsdell's Silver Spring apartment
had been dusted, washed, polished, waxed, generally
spic-and-spanned out of its customary bachelor sloven-
liness. She had hung up carelessly flung clothing. Fresh
flowers stood in twin crystal vases atop the mantle
piece. Despite his grumbling that it was unnecessary,
Mrs. Daly had also ironed the curtains and shampooed
the living room rug.

The place looked immaculate, Ramsdell was forced
to admit. Just right for a wedding. Idly, he wondered if
the butterflies chasing each other around inside his
stomach resulted from the wingding the "Irregulars"
had surprised him with the night before, the naturally
queasy feeling a thirty-five year old man had shortly
before an initial plunge into matrimony, or a combination of both.

At length, Ramsdell could speculate no more, because time, as is its habit, ran out. At two o'clock, the
first guest arrived. Afterwards, the doorbell rang constantly, the apartment filled, the initial buzz and hum
of conversation and laughter became a rising roar from
a wall-to-wall sea of people.

Laura, radiantly beautiful in blue. Henry Maddox.
Kent Grayson. Barney Lippert and the entire Brain
Drain, Inc. crew. Alonzo Cole. Timmy Benjamin. Dr.
Klein from the Public Health Service. Ramsdell's
brother and father. Laura's mother and older sister.

Promptly at four, Roy and Laura stood before Federal Judge Owen Crandall, a college classmate of the

senior Ramsdell. Crandall, whose reputation for "keeping things moving in his courtroom" was legendary around Washington, performed the ceremony in much the same manner.

Cutting the wedding cake, his hand over his bride's on the handle of the knife, Ramsdell leaned closer, whispered to Laura, "Too late now, darling. The deed is done. You're inextricably hooked up with a guy who spends most of his waking hours draped over a computer, keeps no set schedule, and might stay at the office two or three days if he's bogged down in the middle of a project. Doesn't that scare you even a little bit?"

She shook her head, laughing gaily. "I just hope you can program and read printouts better than you're hacking up this poor unoffending cake, Roy. And by the way, when did you last catch a doctor punching a time clock? Oh, Roy, I'm so happy!"

Finally, after the mandatory champagne and thrown rice, tearful parents and last-minute kisses, Roy and Laura escaped the throng of well-wishers into their car.

En route to the airport, where they planned to emplane for a Hawaiian honeymoon, Roy Ramsdell smiled the smile of a satisfied, fulfilled human being. Laura snuggled contentedly against his shoulder.

"A penny, Roy," she said, brushing her lips against his ear.

"For my thoughts? They're worth a hell of a lot more now. Millions, Mrs. Ramsdell. Important things like sun and surf and sand and ten marvelous days at the Ilikai devoted to fun and games with my brand new wife."

"Not nearly enough, Roy," Laura breathed. "Just the beginning. I want a lifetime of that."

She was right, of course, Ramsdell reflected. He wanted the same. A lifetime in a world returned to normal, one in which the refugees had gone back to their homes, underground shelters and protective clothing could be forgotten, the Panama Canal and the Rio Grande were fast-fading memories, a nation might bind up its wounds and go about the business of living again.

Epilogue

On his sorghum, soybean and peanut farm three miles southwest of Searcy, Arkansas, Chester Looney braked his heavy-duty John Deere tractor to a halt, allowing the motor to idle, as he took a break from his task of plowing the rich black soil of his lower forty.

Looney fanned his sweating face with a straw hat that had seen better days, tapped a toe in time to the wailing country music guitars wafting from a portable radio taped to the tractor's frame. Suddenly, a new sound intruded—a high-pitched, whining buzz. Looney slapped with annoyance at his neck, screeched in surprised anger when a painful, stinging dart entered his flesh just behind the left ear.

The farmer's eyes followed a fat, inch-long, orange-and-black object that, having eluded his attempt at annihilation, rose waveringly into the air, gained altitude and was soon lost from view against the setting sun.

• • •

The bee found its destination, a hive in a small tree where it sought the queen, who was ready to receive him. Soon there were more hybrids . . .

Thrilling, mind-expanding novels
science fiction's most prestigious autho

The TEMPO Science Fiction Library

——12126 **THE WEAPON MAKERS**
A. E. Van Vogt ($1.25)
One man decides a monumental battle between The Weapon Shops and an entire empire. "One of the all-time greats!"—*Fantasy & Science Fiction*

——12127 **PLANETS FOR SALE**
A. E. Van Vogt and E. Mayne Hull ($1.25)
In a future where tycoons joust for control of a galaxy, the enigmatic Artur Blord, idealist, scoundrel, and financial wizard, fights for power and for love.

——12128 **EIGHTEEN GREATEST SCIENCE FICTION STORIES** Laurence M. Janifer, ed. ($1.50)
The greatest science fiction writers' own choice of the greatest science fiction stories ever written. With stories by Bradbury, Heinlein, Sturgeon, and 15 other masters.

——12129 **VOYAGERS IN TIME**
Robert Silverberg, ed. ($1.25)
A Hugo Award Winner's superb collection of twelve time travel stories by H. G. Wells, Bester, del Rey, among others.

——12130 **MINDS UNLEASHED**
Groff Conklin, ed. ($1.25)
The incredible powers of human intelligence are the theme of this fascinating anthology. A dozen stories by Clarke, Leinster, Tenn, Asimov, and other greats.

——12131 **GREAT STORIES OF SPACE TRAVEL**
Groff Conklin, ed. ($1.25)
The shores of space explored by eleven notables, including Vance, del Rey, Knight, and Clarke.

TEMPO—BOOK MAILING SERVICE
BOX 1050, ROCKVILLE CENTRE, N.Y. 11571

————Send me—FREE!—your current TEMPO BOOKS catalog listing hundreds of books.

Please send me the books I have checked above. I am enclosing $————. (Please add 25¢ to total to cover postage and handling.) Send check or money order; no cash or C.O.D.'s accepted.

(Please Print)

Name————————————————————————

Address——————————————————————

City————————————State————Zip————
Please allow three weeks for delivery.